The Guild

The Guild

Michael Gill

iUniverse, Inc.
New York Bloomington

The Guild

iUniverse books may be ordered through booksellers or by contacting:

iUniverse
1663 Liberty Drive
Bloomington, IN 47403
www.iuniverse.com
1-800-Authors (1-800-288-4677)

ISBN: 978-0-595-53526-2 (pbk)
ISBN: 978-0-595-63592-4 (ebk)

Printed in the United States of America

iUniverse rev. date: 1/13/089

Chapter 1

HE STARTED TO REGAIN his senses, at first he just realised that he was awake, and then it suddenly came to him that his eyes were covered. As he tried to move, he soon realised that his arms and legs were bound to a board of some sort. His mind began to clear; he could remember, being released from prison. He had thought that the day would never come; the last six years seemed like a lifetime. At that time of his imprisonment, James Sindel had been 23 years old. From the age of eight until he was about 12, he had been molested by a group of paedophiles, some of whom were members of his own family. From leaving school James worked at an assurance office working as a claims adjuster covering household insurance, life insurance and motor insurance. He was 6 ft 1 inch tall, he topped the scales at almost 15 stone, he was always smartly dressed, clean neat and tidy with mousy blonde hair and he gave the appearance of being a respectable member of society. He was quite a large man although he was not what people would call a hard person he had a weak soft face. All his mannerisms tended to lead one to think that maybe he was a bit of a mother's boy or even a little bit gay. James spent a lot of time with the local Boy Scouts movement; in fact, he ran the local cub group. This is where he groom children for himself and his little group of like-minded friends. Around the age of 20 he discovered that he liked enjoying children for his sexual pleasures and his sadistic tendency went to such an extent that he found it necessary to kill most of them when he had finally finished with them. By the time he went to prison, he and his little group were responsible for the deaths of 15 children. James felt no remorse for any of his actions; he was one of those people that believed that he had a superior brain giving him a superior intelligence compared to anybody else. He saw no reason why what he was doing to the children, could be considered wrong, he really believed that they enjoyed what he and his friends were doing. Even if they did not like it, what did it matter he and his friends were so clever that they never expected to be caught. He really could not see that what he and his friends were doing was wrong. He could see no reason why being the superior person that he was he should not just do as he pleased anyway.

Walking through the gates of the prison on the day that he was released he was thinking that at the first chance that he got he would find himself a child. He would make that child suffer for the last six years of pain, just the same as he had suffered. It was of no matter to him if it was a boy or a girl, he was not in the mood to spend time grooming a youngster he just wanted to be the one in charge again. As he turned the first corner, he almost collided with a middle-aged man jogging in a tracksuit. It was going through his mind what an idiot this person was he was no spring chicken and to be jogging at his age was really being stupid. Suddenly everything had gone black.

How could he have been so careless? Why had he allowed his guard to slip so quickly? James Sindel had learnt in the last six years to keep his wits about him, never walk into an empty room or enclosed space. If he did, he could expect trouble. Even the guards had no liking for him although the guards sometimes pulled the other inmates off him they always took their time and accidentally managed to inflict an extra bit of pain on him. He also learnt to make himself as inconspicuous as possible. By doing this and a few more things that he preferred to forget, he managed to come under the protection of one of the hardest men in the prison.

As he lay in a state of almost full awareness he realise that he was not lying on boards he was in fact hanging from them. He also suddenly realise that he was naked! In the last six years, plenty of violent and nasty things had happened to James Sindel. They had all been beyond his control and in that six years he'd come to realise that people that caused him the most trouble really did believe that he deserved it. When he had left the prison, he believed that all this was behind him and that his nightmare had ended.

He was now fully awake and terrified that maybe the nightmare was going to start all over again. He had learned a lot about fear in the last six years. For the first nine months, all that happened to him were beatings any time that somebody got the chance to hurt him he got hurt. He suffered broken fingers, arms, ribs and once two men tried to break both his legs the fact that they only managed to heavily bruise him was pure luck on his part because, it was one of the few times that the wardens stepped in before too much damage could be done. He had been hurt with razor blades, broken china with anything that they could make into a weapon. In that nine months so much happened to him that he was beginning to believe that he would never live long enough to finish his sentence. A few months later, he would have accepted death as a welcome relief from what he had to do.

One day he was resting on his bed in his cell when the door crashed open, James curled up into a ball waiting for yet another beating. Joe Ralph stood over James shaking his head.

"I think it's time we stopped people beating you up."

James kept quiet and waited for that first blow to land; to his way of thinking if the beatings were; going to stop that meant that Joe had come to kill him. Joe Ralph was a convicted murderer sentenced to life imprisonment, two years into his sentence he had managed to escape and promptly killed two of the witnesses that put him in jail in the first place. He received another life sentence, a year later he killed an inmate for interrupting him while he was reading one of his comics. Joe was not very bright but he was very hard, very violent and sometimes he could read words that had more than two syllables. For this last act of violence, Joe received a further life sentence with no parole. This punishment was probably one of the stupidest things that the law could have done. Joe being rather thick found prison life quite comfortable, He had no decisions to make, his food supplied three times a day without any effort on his part, and the fact that he was a man that was now untouchable, as the worst punishment they could give him now was solitary. If he did wrong, all that would happen was the loss of his privileges and he was big enough and hard enough to take what he needed from the other inmates.

"Now listen to me Sindel," Joe said.

"I have decided that I will help you. I am about the only person in this jail that can stop the other blokes knocking you about. You will become my slave. You will do what I tell you to do when I tell you to do it and how I tell you to do it. When I need a wank you do it, when my prick needs sucking you suck it?"

James, mind was in turmoil, this was not a matter of him choosing or not choosing to agree to a suggestion from Joe, he had no choice to make. Joe was telling not asking and to argue would mean James death. James liked sex with children he had never had any sexual relationship with a grown-up, either a man or woman. The very idea of it was repulsive to James. However, James believing he had a superior brain and was 10 times cleverer than Joe decided that if he submitted then he would probably work his way out of most of those nasty duties.

"OK Joe I'll do it. Even that's got to be better than living like I am now."

After the first few weeks when the novelty for Joe of having a slave had worn off, Joe put James to work, he had become Joe's sex toy. Although Joe was one of the hardest men in the prison well known for violence, he was not a mean man with his toys. Joe took great pleasure in the fact that he was always happy to share his toy with any one who was willing to pay a token price. Joes price for James favours was simple, one cigarette one cum, and it did not matter how the sex toy made you cum. By his hands or his mouth in made no difference if you used his arse, the price was always the same, one cum one cigarette, or as Joe put it with great peels of laughter "a fag for a fag." James never understood the thinking behind Joe's mind. Joe was a child when two men that looked similar to James abused him. This had left him with a terrible hatred of kiddie fiddlers and this was Joe's way of getting revenge on his abusers. James came to hate Joe but most of all he feared him, he was made to wear make-up and he had to effect a feminine mincing walk and voice but worst of all were the times that Joe rented him out for gang bangs, sometimes up to 10 men at a time. James was earning Joe enough cigarettes each day for Joe to become a very heavy smoker. In time James, learn to cope with his arse used by anybody with a spare cigarette, and a hard on. What really made him sick at heart were the blow jobs, it was bad enough having a man's prick in his mouth, using it like a woman's pussy but most of the men were dirty, they seldom washed their pricks before pushing his head into their laps. The smell and taste of these men used to give him nightmares. Most of the men were quite indifferent to him while he was sucking their pricks until they were about to cum, then they took great delight in making him swallow their muck.

His thoughts came to a halt by a voice, a cold hard voice that put so much fear into him that his bowels just let go. The shit flew away from his body like a fountain it hit the boards above him and ran across his back and legs. He screamed as the tape ripped from his eyes taking most of his eyebrows and eye lashes with it; he could see the shit splashing on the floor beneath him. He remembered that voice; he remembered what that voice had said to him before he was bundled into the prison van that started his journey into hell. That voice had stayed with him for the last six years it was always in his nightmares, and they were many. That voice, that flat cold bitter voice that had spoken each word as if being carved into stone.

"I will wait for you to come out, and when you do I will kill you so slowly, that you will feel as much pain as my grandchildren did, and feel as much fear as they did, I'll go to the ends of the earth to see you die." At that time, although it had frightened him he never thought he would have to face that man again.

"James fucking Sindel I have waited six fucking years for your release from prison. Time has healed no wounds for me, I fucking hate and despise you more now than I fucking did when I discovered what you and your kiddie fiddling friends had done to my grandchildren. To me you are worth less than the fucking shit that has just fallen from your arse. You are the scum of the earth; you have lost the right to common justice or the right to live. The law found you, took you to court and proved you guilty and then they still only gave you six fucking years. That is not fucking justice that is a travesty. Six years for the lives of two young children, I will fucking well show you what justice is. You refused to give up the names of the people that were with you when you killed my grandchildren; you have protected that fucking scum for six years. I attended the funeral of my grandchildren I also watched the break-up of my daughter's marriage. I then had to see her suffer a nervous breakdown and three attempted suicides. Now I will have justice. You are going to give me the names of the men that molested and killed my grandchildren. Have no doubt in your mind; you will give me the fucking names." The fear that James felt at these words made him vomit. He knew that he was in more danger than he had ever been in all the six years of prison life. The fact that his eyes had been taped shut was the only glimmer of hope that he had because up to the he had only heard the voice. He had not actually seen his attacker and if his attacker kept out of his line of sight then there was a chance that he was going to be set free at some point. If he did not see his attacker then it made sense that he would be alive when this was over. He would be alive maybe even crippled but he would be alive and he would not be able to identify anybody. Maybe he was only going to be beaten, OK he might have a few bones broken and maybe that would satisfy his attacker. He had survived many beatings by people that were used to violent attacks compared to them his attacker would be a beginner. If he kept his head, he thought that he could still outwit this man. After all, he knew the man and he knew that he was better educated and that he had a superior brainpower.

He could hear the man moving around the room, he started to think them maybe he could talk his way out to this. In prison, the beatings had come quickly without warning, no words, just fists and boots. This man was in no hurry. People can plan things that include great violence but when it comes to it, their natural sense of behaviour and their conscience would hold them back. It takes either a sick mind or someone with no conscience or feelings for a man to inflict real violent pain on another. James reasoned that this man by his lack of haste was not up to it. It seemed to James that he was trying to work himself up to it, or he was possibly playing a part just to frighten James into telling him what he wanted to know. James brain was working overtime now; he was convinced that he had the mark of the man.

Although his words were hard James reasoned that Follet, for he knew this man to be Follet the grandfather of the two kids that had been responsible for him going to prison, had over the years allowed his anger to weaken. The pain must have dulled by now; the man had had six years to come to terms with the loss of those two snotty nosed kids. From what he could remember of Ken Follet, he was a normal working stiff, not a hardened killer, not like Joe Ralph or any of the dozen men that had been fucking his arse for years. Yes, everything would be OK, he had the brains to get out of this and he could out think a man like Ken Follet any fucking day of the week. Everything was going to be OK. James could feel the man getting nearer; he could feel the hot breath of the man against his naked skin. The pain that came was sharp, the small craft knife had been pushed into his left-arm and drawn down from shoulder to elbow the cut was only a quarter of an inch deep but the shock had been immense. James screams of pain and fear echoed around the room he could see his blood splashing on the floor beneath him. He started to understand that maybe he had misjudged Ken Follet.

Ken Follet laughed; he had waited six years for this moment, six years of mental hell. The deaths of his two grandchildren at the hands of a group of paedophiles plus the shock of the investigation and the trial of James Sindel were enough to disrupt any sane person's mind. Add to that the breakdown and three attempted suicides of his daughter it would not surprise anyone to find that his thirst for vengeance had been eating away at his brain and his personality.

The hatred that he fell for this man bored into his mind like a worm into a ripe apple. After the trial, Ken Follet had sold his house and converted everything he owned to cash. Then he had moved to a city a few hundred miles away from his hometown. That was when he changed his name to Max Keller. He had chosen this name at random from the telephone book. He was then 45 years old and as far as he was concerned, his life was over. Since then he had lived purely for revenge, his aim was to wait until James came out from prison and then he would make James pay for what he had done. If he could get James to give up the names of the other men involved with his grandchildren's deaths then he would have his revenge in full. Up until then he had been a law abiding average citizen now he had decided that he would become judge, jury and executioner. He wanted old justice,

An eye for an eye, a tooth for a tooth. He intended to make sure that they suffered more than anyone had ever suffered before, to his mind this would give a warning to all kiddie fiddlers, also it might make ordinary people start to react against these pounces. In the last six years, he had kept his head down and kept away from trouble he had been so nondescript that not more than a few people even knew that he existed. Only about three of them would be able to give an accurate description of him, it was as if he never registered in people's minds. He kept on the move taking only cash-in-hand jobs, living in grotty cheep lodgings and all of the time planning his revenge, he was now a man who had come to terms with the fact that he no longer had a life that was worth living. The only thoughts in his mind were of vengeance and more vengeance; the worms of hatred spend all day eating the apple from the inside out. He had lived and breathed for revenge all this time and he had gone through dozens of ways in which he could get James to talk. Finely he had worked out a method that would not only give him the information that he wanted but also a way to make sure that James underwent the most amount of pain that was possible. He could see nothing wrong with the fact that he was intending to take another person's life, his mind had slipped so far that he considered what he was doing was a favour for mankind.

His world had been shattered. Max had gone from being a happy widower with a beautiful daughter married to a man that he not only admired but also truly liked. He had two wonderful grandchildren who thought the world of him. With his good health and a good job working as an assistant in a hardware shop, he had changed to an angry hate-filled loner with only revenge to keep him half-sane. He lived only for revenge now. Max had always been reasonably bright with a lot of common sense. He still was, he knew that the way he was acting and feeling was not normal but his lust for revenge cancelled all thoughts of right and wrong from his mind. He was going to kill James Sindel very slowly.

When James eyes stopped watering and he regained the ability to focus properly he tried to look round the room, he could not see a lot because of his head was strapped tightly to the board, but at last, he was starting to think a lot better. He strained to look at his surroundings thinking that if he did manage to get away with his life. Then anything he could remember might help to catch this lunatic. He was worried now that Ken had uncovered his eyes, being able to see meant that James could give the police a description of his attacker. Thinking of the times that he had taken children without planning James remembered that the only time that he had let any of his chance victims see his face was when he had already decided to kill them.

Still Ken was just a working stiff, that sort of person should be used to being a loser. He would never summon up the guts to go through with a killing, killing another human. Although most people thought about it at one time or another in their lives, it was not something that sat easily on the conscience of the normal working person. He would still get out of this, after all; he was far cleverer than any fucking shop assistant was, any day of the week. From what he could see of the room, it was not really a room after all it was a large empty workshop with tiled walls and tiled floor. By moving his head as much as the restraints would let him he could see his outstretched arms with two leather straps binding each to the large wooden board that must have been suspended from the ceiling. Although he could not see his legs, they felt secured in the same manner as his arms. He could also feel a leather strap across his forehead which restricted his head movements, there was also two strong straps one across his hips and one across his chest the straps held James in such a position that he could only move about a very small amount. He was left facing a floor with his arms and legs out stretched as if he was skydiving, his wrists were twisted round so it palms of his hands were facing the wood. The board raised above the ground with a block and tackle by about 7 ft directly underneath him he could see two puddles one was the shit that he had lost earlier and the other was a puddle of his vomit mixed with his own blood.

Although James was naturally arrogant he was not stupid he knew that he was in a lot of trouble and he now realise that he was down to suffer a bit more than a normal beating. The thought kept coming into his head that he would get out of this by using his brains. However, by looking at the two puddles on the floor he had to admit that so far this man's tactics were making a good job of frightening him. By straining his head as much as possible, he could just see a wooden table with a small barbecue on it that was a light. As he managed to focus properly on the table, he could see some tools laid out. A large hammer, a bunch of six-inch nails, which he thought used to secure the leather straps to the board. The other three objects bought a cold sweat to James. They were a set of bolt croppers, a chain saw and a can of petrol. James started to sob and then his sobbing turn to screams as he realise that in the barbecue a large flat bar of metal was heating up in the hot coals. He now began to have doubts about getting out of this situation alive.

Before he was frightened, but now he was terrified. James screamed,

"I know who you arc Ken Follet you'll never get away with this. You are the first person they will look for. You let me go now and I promise that I will say nothing to anyone about this, I promise, I promise, I promise on my mother's life, I promise, I swear to God I promise." James was now sobbing so much that his chest hurt. A wooden chair slid into James's view, Max or as James knew him Ken Follet came and sat down, he looked at James for a long time with a cold hard stare. There was no mercy, in fact there was no emotion in Max at all there had not been any for six years. Max had changed in the last six years. His fair short hair was now long and straggly and along with his eyebrows and a new beard. This dyed jet-black with a few little streaks of grey in them. This was a drastic change from his naturally well-groomed fair hair and clean looks of six years ago. Sitting down, as he was, James did not notice that Max was wearing inserts in his shoes giving him another two inches on his 5 ft 10 inches in height. Max held a note pad and pen,

"I want the names of the rest of your group, those that you have protected all this time." James by now realised that if he gave up the names then there was no chance that he would stay alive, so he said

"Fucking go to hell, you fucking bastard, I will tell you nothing." Max could see that James was overcoming his fear, not by much, this was not good. He needed to get the pace going a little bit faster, the last thing he wanted was for James to have any time to think about what was happening.

"You have no fucking choice, you tell me now or later, I have all the time in the world. I have rented this old workshop for another seven days. How much pain do you want before you finally tell me what happened to my grandchildren and the names of the people that helped you to do it? Tell me now and save yourself from what's about to happen to you." James said nothing, Max rose from the chair and went to the table, when he returned he held the hammer and two nails, James started to sweat again but said nothing.

The first nail drove through the back of James left hand into the wood; this was no timid attack, the nail six inches long, hammered in until the head was flush with the skin on the back of James's hand.

"Give me the names." the voice was flat, cold with no emotion in it. James was screaming but all he said was

"You fucking bastard." the second nail went right through the back of James right hand.

"Names." said Max, to his surprise he felt nothing he had planned this for years right down to the last detail, it gave him no feeling of joy or satisfaction, no feeling at all in fact. James continued to scream but said nothing.

Max sat on the chair and rolled a cigarette. Even in his pain, James noted the fact that Max was using Golden Virginia tobacco. He even managed a bid of satisfaction when he saw Max used a filter tip, at least the man was worried about his health, maybe later the police could get some DNA from the filter tip. It also helped him to believe the Max was an ordinary working bloke. Max sat back and smoked a cigarette he was waiting for the pain in James hands to subside. He knew that too much pain all at once and James would pass out. Max sat and watched drips of blood as they formed two small pools on the floor in line with James's hands. James hung suspended from the board sobbing quietly; he just could not believe this was happening to him. Through his tears, he could also see the two pools of blood and he could see a puddle of piss.

Max rose to his feet, the hammer swung upwards James started screaming as the end of his right index finger exploded in a sudden burst of pain. The hammer had crushed the nail bed and bone at the end of the finger the pain was horrendous the screams echoed round the workshop. In all his plans, Max had considered James to be a weak-minded person, somebody intimidated by the violence he had suffered. He would give up the names that Max wanted, then Max intended to cut him a few times and watch him bleed to death. Max was fast changing his mind about James's ability to absorb all this pain. The screams had subsided to a low whimper.

"Give me the fucking names and let's have an ending to this." To Max's surprise the answer came in quite a firm voice

"Fuck you, you mother fucking bastard. I will tell you nothing. If you're going to kill me then get on with it!" The hammer flew upwards repeatedly, and yet again James screams were even louder than before. Three more fingers on his right hand had the nails crushed to a pulp.

"Names" barked Max.

"Bollocks" screamed back James. That was when Max's mind seemed to go off the rails. The hammer moving in four quick hard strokes, Max started to grin as he looked at the four freshly crushed fingers on James's left hand. James shit himself again at the same time he spewed the remains of the content of his stomach onto the floor beneath him. He then passed out. Max, started to giggle then, the giggle turned to laughter the laughter became loud, making the sound that only an insane person can make when they laugh.

When James came round he found that Max had cut the leather strap that held his head against the board, Max had not done this out of kindness he had done it so that James could see the damage that had happened to his hands. The question from Max was the same

"Give me the names." The answer although more subdued was the same

"Get fucked." While waiting for James to regain consciousness Max had cleaned off the hammer and thrown it into a corner.

"I am through playing games with you. Now are you going to give me the names that I want?" still James said nothing, his silence had nothing to do with bravado. He could see the bolt croppers in Max's hands. His terror was so great that he had lost the power of speech. He could imagine what was coming next; he was so terrified that there was no way that he could make his voice work. Max took the silence as bravado on James' part he really could not understand why the man was being so stubborn. At the same time Max found himself in a strange position, he discovered that he was really looking forward to what he was about to do next. He had gone past the stage where sanity rules in most normal people, he now had the power of life-or-death over this man. He was corrupted by it. He had even gone past the stage of really wanting to know the names of the other people and if the truth was known, part of him hoped that James would never tell him and that he could just keep going, snipping bits and pieces off James body. Max had in fact lost any feelings that he had for anyone even his grandchildren he was just enjoying what he was doing. Max was on a very high plane now he had entered into a strange quiet deep-seated madness. He found that he was enjoying inflicting pain on someone else, the power that he now had was more intense than anything he had ever experienced in his life. He walked under James and very slowly and deliberately cut off both of James big toes with the bolt croppers.

The pain that James felt made the rest of his injuries seemed as nothing, as his screams subsided and his eyes began to focus he could see his toes laying among a mixture of vomit, shit, blood and piss that was on the floor beneath him.

"Tell me the names" Max had an evil glint in his eyes, for the very first time since the deaths of his grandchildren, he had a smile of pleasure on not only his lips but also in his eyes.

"Fuck off you mad fucking bastard." James was now crying and whimpering at the same time. Max held out a small mirror so that James could see his own face.

"Is this how the children looked just before you and the other fucking kiddie fiddlers finally snuffed out their little lives? Why did you have to kill them? Answer me that and I will let you live a while longer."

"They had to die" James replied, if only he could live for a few extra moments, then there was a chance that something could happen to alter the situation. His friends were supposed to have met him at the cafe just a little way up the road from the prison. They should be looking for him; if only he could hold out long enough, he would see this bastard go to his maker. What he did not know was the fact that he had been transported fifty miles while he was unconscious, his friends would not know where to look for him.

"They had both been damaged beyond repair, they had seen our faces and could identify us all and because of that they had to die. Surely you must understand that?" If ever a man had used the wrong set of words, this was the time. Max felt a surge of hatred rise up to block out his thoughts all he could think of was to hurt this ruthless killer and inflict as much pain as possible. His plan went out of the window. Pulling the iron bar from the barbecue, he banged it on the floor to remove any bits of charcoal and then walked under James. The Red hot bar came up without warning into contact with James bollocks, the smell of burning flesh was enough to make a normal man sick, Max just smiled and breathed deeply, even above the screams he could still hear the sizzle of flesh against the iron bar as he gradually pushed it deeper into James's groin. It was some moments before Max realised James was no longer screaming James had passed out, once again.

Max sat on the chair and rolled another smoke, by now he had expected to have managed to extract the information that he needed. In all his plans, he never dreamt that James would hold out this long, there was no reason for him to do so. As he sat, he started thinking of his future. Until today, he had not thought he had one. Today had affected him more than he expected it to, he had been prepared to cause James a lot of pain and after that he had been prepared to kill him. After all, in his mind, James deserved to die and Max believed now that he had been given the right to carry out that particular type of justice. What Max had not prepared for was the thrill, the high that he was getting; he was really looking forward to the next part. He was now coming to believe that he had a natural ability for this sort of thing. That was when the beginnings of an idea started to form in his mind.

Max sat quietly thinking while he smoked three more cigarettes, gradually James regained consciousness and it was obvious to Max that James reserves of strength when now very low. James also knew that his reserves were low he also knew he couldn't go on much longer and he realise that it was now more-or-less too late for any rescue by his friends. He now understood that he was going to get no mercy from Max, all he could expect from that quarter was a slow painful death.

"Are you now ready to give me those fucking names?" Max had the pen and paper ready.

"Bollocks you can rot in hell." this was not the answer that Max was expecting he was sure that he had James beaten. He threw down the pen and pad, and then the knife seemed to appear in his hand as if by magic, it flashed twice in the light, James braced himself for more pain but none came. Max had cut the leather straps that held James wrists to the board. Taking his time Max walked slowly to the corner of the workshop where a door led to the toilet. Max stood pissing into the pan, he could not work out what was happening to James he just could not understand it. How can a man endure so much pain when in theory a few names would have stopped in all? Max began to realise that after you have inflicted so much pain on to a human, maybe they become immune to any extra pain. He knew James would scream and cry and all the rest of it but would any of it hurt him more than he had already been hurt. Max soon gave up this chain of thought the man was going to die.

James hung from the board trying to control the violent shaking that was racking his body, he had suffered some terrible injuries and he knew that things were going to get even worse. He had not seen Max return but the sound of a petrol engine starting pulled him back to his full senses. Total horror gripped him as Max approached with the chainsaw.

"Last chance, kiddie fiddler." James did not know why but some sudden stupid streak in him just could not give up the names of his group. There was no reason why he should not, after all the pain that he had been put through nobody would blame him for weakening and telling Max, what he wanted. It was not as if he really liked the others, but he was damned if he was going to give in. It was a very strange time for him suddenly to develop a backbone. He could see the blade of a chain saw now spinning round; his senses had become so sharp that he could see each tooth of the blade as if it were going in real slow motion. The smoke from the petrol engine was obscuring Max's face. All James could see was the blade of the chainsaw. Then Max's face seemed to appear as a ghost among the smoke, this was the first time that he had looked closely at that face, lined with early old age caused by stress and worry but it was looking at those eyes, they told James that he was going to die, but not yet. James started to scream even before the chainsaw started to hack its way through his left wrist. Max took his time about amputating James hand, he wanted to making it last as long as possible. James now knew why there had been two straps on each arm and he now understood why Max had cut the first ones round his wrists. James now believed that Max fully intended to cut off both his hands and both his feet and then gradually work up his arms and legs. First, there would be cuts across his elbows and then across his knees he was going to be hacked to death very slowly and it would appear that the only way out was if he could manage to bleed to death before he suffered too much more pain. The blood was flowing from the stump of James left wrist, James tried with all his mental brainpower to force the blood to flow quicker so that he would die quickly. Max had obviously also thought about James bleeding to death, this was something he did not want to happen, not just yet. Max walked over to the table and withdrew the iron bar from the barbecue. Now James realised what the iron bar was really for. James was barely able to scream any more his throat was red raw and bone-dry. Max used the red-hot iron bar to stem the flow of blood from James wrist there was no way that Max was going to let him bleed to death before he wanted it to happen. For a long time the stench of burnt flesh filled the air, but the blood did stop flowing. Max really did not want James to bleed to death now. Amid the pain in James mind, his brain was working flat out. James had decided to find a way to die quickly. He now knew that there was no way he was going to get out of this alive and even if he could would he really want to. If he told Max the names of people that were in his group, Max would probably not believe him, and would just carry on cutting bits off him, what he needed to do was to make Max so angry and disappointed that he would lose his temper and kill him quickly.

"It's no good for Christ's sake, having the names will not help you, you can't get them now they are all out of your reach." James babbled between screams.

"What the fuck do you mean you fucking bastard? I shall find them with or without your help." Max could suddenly feel his plans going wrong. James started to laugh insanely, laughter and sobbing at the same time, if that is possible.

"After I was arrested and tried my friends got frightened, three of them went straight out to Cuba. Four days after their arrival all three of them died in a car smash, the other two were always the weak ones of our group and they decided rightly or wrongly that you or your family had been the cause of the deaths of the four in Cuba. As they could not face going to prison and were terrified of the fact that you might catch up with them, both decided that there was only one-way out, they both committed suicide. I am the only one who is still alive. So if you really want them, then you can go to hell where they will be waiting for you, and the sooner you fucking join them the fucking better." For some reason Max fully believed that James was telling the truth, he figured that the man was far too gone to be lying to him. He now knew that his lust for vengeance against his grandchildren's killers was over. Max left James hanging from the palate while he carried the bolt croppers, hammer and chainsaw to the toilet, the iron bar he dropped in the pool of blood and shit that was on the floor. He left James hanging from the palate; James was whimpering and crying but even so he could hear the hot iron sizzling as the blood and vomit cooled it down.

In the toilet, Max rinsed the tools off in warm soapy water to remove any fingerprints left on them. On his return to where James was hanging he put them back on the table and then dragged the table underneath James. James was now a jabbering sobbing wreck screaming and muttering words that Max could not make out, in fact the events of the day had finally driven James mad.

"Right you scumbag, I've given you what you deserve. I am now through with you. Your life is now over. I sincerely fucking hope that you fucking go to hell. I hope there you will suffer for all the young children that you and your friends killed over and over for the rest of eternity." He them piled James' clothes on top of the tools, collapsed the table so that it laid among the shit and blood on the floor directly underneath James, then he poured petrol from and the petrol can over everything on the table. Once again, the knife appeared as by magic. He reached out and his hand moved, James was screaming with pain even before he saw what remained of his prick lying on top of the pile of clothes soaked in petrol. James could not believe that one man could do so much damage to a fellow human being. Max made the second cut this time he opened James stomach from one side to the other. He watched as James guts hung down nearly to the pile of clothes, he intended to watch James bleed to death. As James lifeblood was dripping away Max went back to the toilet and had a shower, when he finished he put his old clothes and shoes into a carrier bag, he opened another carrier bag that contained his new fresh clothes. He was now dressed clean and tidy as if he had been out for an evening stroll, carrying the bag he went back to James. As he stood watching the last of James blood leave his body he rolled a cigarette, James was really close to death now In fact he was almost gone.

"I hope you fucking rot in hell." James heard these last words before he died.

Max then threw the lighted match on to the petrol-soaked clothes and walked out of the workshop.

Chapter 2

Detective Inspector Adam Davies started life as an awkward child after taking nine hours on the delivery table he finally entered this world as a 7lb 10oz screaming red faced bundle. He had been awkward all his life. In his late teens, he became very friendly with a young good-looking lad called Geoffrey Balcombe. This was the start of a long friendship, which most people suspected to be more than just friendly. Adam was nearly 35 before he realise that being a homosexual would hold his career back in the police force. To rectify matters he quickly lost Jeffrey and married a woman called Bernadette who had the appearance of a real live living doll, unfortunately she had the same sort of brainpower. To say that this was a marriage of convenience would be putting it mildly. Adam now had the required little wife at home that could turn out for functions whenever needed, Bernadette had a husband with a promising career and quite good money, she also had an husband with a very low sex drive which left her plenty of time and energy for all the nice young men that Adam worked with. Adam had reached the rank of detective inspector with the CID, although he was not liked by his superiors or the people that worked under him, he was a very capable detective, often getting results that other members of the CID could not manage to do. The main reason that he was not liked was the fact that although he proved himself a very hard forthright person and thief taker, he came across as very cold and standoffish. He kept himself to himself and he seemed to have no friends in the force as he always gave the impression that he wanted nothing to do with his work colleagues once a day's work had finished. Adam spoke with a slow West Country accent that gave the people that he was talking to the impression that he was half-asleep and perhaps a little bit dozy, in fact, Adam had a very sharp intelligent mind and he had a tenacity that made him feared by most criminals in his area.

Adam stood in the middle of the workshop shaking his head. It was not often that any scene of crime that he came across could upset his stomach, but now he was having a hard job to keep his supper where it belonged. In all his experience, he had never seen anything so brutal and deliberate. The body hanging from the block and tackle, had been so badly mutilated that it was hard for him to imagine how much pain that man must have suffered before he died. At first glance, Adam could see no obvious details that would lead him to the killer or killers. It had been sheer luck that they had this much evidence left to see as it was. There were not many old age pensioners that not only walk their dogs at this time of night in such a low-lit area and not many of them that carried a mobile phone. Jack Foster had been walking his dog towards run-down buildings and noticed a man who appeared to be leaving by the door at the side. At the same time, he could see what looked like the flicker of flames through one of the side windows. Not wishing to confront the man that was leaving, Jack waited until the man was a good distance away. Then he entered the building by pushing open the door. Looking around he found a fire extinguisher and tried to use on the fire, naturally the kids had already been in there and found the extinguisher and emptied it just for fun. Adam admired the old man's spirit he had used the extinguisher to push the pile of burning objects from beneath the body, he then called the ambulance and the police. Jack Foster gave a description of the man leaving the building as about six feet tall with black hair and a dark beard, dressed in a jacket and trousers. He admitted that it was not much of a description. He had only seen the man for a few seconds and that had been from a distance. A young police officer stepped through the doorway to tell Adam that the forensic people were now here. He took one look at the body with the contents of the stomach hanging almost to the floor and promptly spewed his heart out. Adam stood back to let the forensic people do their job. He knew that this was going to be a very tough case and that the press would have a field day with this one.

This was a sheer brutal killing. Naturally, they would eventually manage to identify the body but until then he had absolutely nothing to go on. As he stood there, he summed up the few facts that he had. A lonely piece of ground, old run-down factory, a few fire damaged tools, some half-burnt clothes, a very badly mutilated body and a very vague description of a man who might or might not have had anything to do with the case. In addition, just to put the cream on the cake that description could fit half the men in England. Adam realised that in the next few weeks he was going to take a lot of hard abuse not only from the press but from his governors as well.

Chapter 3

AT THE TIME OF James, imprisonment Ken was 45 years old. Ken was a nice man, helpful considerate, and always willing to listen to other people's problems, Ken was religious, but not overly so. 17 years previously, Ken and his wife Jean with their daughter Mary were driving through a town when a joy rider in a stolen car roared out of a side street. He was being chased by a police car. The joy riders car smashed into the side of their car. Ken and his daughter Mary, were unhurt sadly, the accent killed Jean. The young 14-year-old lad that was behind the wheel of the stolen car also died. It took many years for Ken to get over the death of his wife. It was the fact that he had to bring up Mary who was then eight that pulled him through the bad times. Mary had grown up to be an intelligent young woman she was both kind and considerate, Ken and Mary had developed a kind of special bond over the years that can only be formed between a father and his daughter when there is no mother present. The bond was so great that they virtually worshipped each other. The day that Mary got married was both one of the happiest and saddest days in Ken's life. He was so happy to see her make a good match and at the same time so sad that his wife Jean could not be there to see her daughter blossom into a full-grown woman. Mary had two children a boy and a girl. As they grew, so they became Ken's whole life and existence, he worshipped the ground that they walked on, when the boy told his grandfather that he wanted to join the cub's Ken was thrilled to bits.

Ken never quite trusted James when he became the leader of the pack. He could not put his finger on anything in particular but he just was not happy with something in the man's attitude. However, he never suspected the truth. Ken's world started to fall to pieces the day his grandchildren went missing, after five days Ken was so distraught and worried that he would have given his own life just to see the children back. The strain on his daughter and her husband was terrible. When the bodies of the children were found, that was when Mary's first breakdown started to happen. They had been badly beaten, mutilated and were naked, dumped in a skip in black dustbin sacks. Mary made the first attempt at her own life. Her husband a good man and fine father to the children just could not understand fully what was happening to his world, unfortunately he just could not take it. One night he got into his car and drove it straight into a local canal. Ken went into a very deep depression he turned against religion entirely, and he became surly and mean-spirited. Three months later evidence found in James flat linked him into the deaths of the children. During the trial Ken could not believe the way that James behaved, to listen to the man you would have thought that he had done those children a favour, he showed no remorse and also he would not give up the names of his associates he was sent to prison for six years with no remission.

On the day, that James started his prison sentence Ken sat down with a bottle of whisky and started to plan what he was going to do. Halfway through the night Max Keller was invented. The name was picked at random from the phone book; there was not any sort of thought that went into the name. All that Ken knew about false names was that it was a mistake made by many criminals when picking a false name to keep their original initials. Ken knew what he was going to do, and he knew he would be breaking the law. He did not intend to be discovered so he had decided on a completely new identity. It was a means for him to get his revenge. From that, moment on the only time he used his original name was when he sold his house. Max as he now called himself sold everything and converted it all to hard cash; he had set up a trust fund for Mary so that she would be looked after, as by now she was incapable of looking after herself. She had had two more breakdowns and had tried more than once to kill herself. Maybe one day he would be able to come back and see her, any thought of this was a long shot at the moment there appeared to be no way that she would recover from the depths of depression that she'd been plunged into. Doing what he planned too, he could see no way that he would be either in prison or dead. He had come to reconciled himself to the fact that he would never see his daughter again. With all his possessions which now consisted basically of a bag of money Max got on a train and moved to a large town a few hundred miles away. Max spent the first eight weeks in a backstreet lodging house. In that time he let his hair grow and he grew a beard, once the hair had grown Max moved to a different lodging house, between moving lodging houses he died his hair and beard jet-black with a little grey. This made him look much older. Max now looked entirely different from the assistant in the hardware shop, were he had worked for many years. It is doubtful if any of his customers would have recognised him. He was no longer the clean-shaven happy go lucky man with near blonde hair standing 5 ft 10 inches tall. Now he had built up shoes that made him 6 ft tall he kept his hair scruffy, he also brought some dark brown contact lenses he was now a very different looking man.

Over the next few weeks, Max started several bank accounts. He travelled from town to town to make him harder to trace, using several different names and security details to set up these accounts. He wasn't sure if it was true or not but he had heard that if you have more than £10,000 in a bank account then the bank automatically informed the taxman, Ken didn't take any chances so he kept each account underneath that. To make sure that he would not forget where the money was or which identity he had used for each bank. He made a list of all the details opened one final account with a small bank and left the details in a small packet with them. He had put adequate money into the account to cover the bank charges for a good many years. Max Keller now had to wait patiently and without causing trouble or getting himself notice for James Sindels release from jail.

Chapter 4

As he made his way back to his lodgings, Max stopped at the chemist and bought three different sets of medicine to cover the symptoms of flu. Then he put on a hangdog expression so when he returned to the House that he was renting a room in, the property owner fully believed that he was suffering from the flue and she understood him when he said he would probably not be out of his room for a few days. He could still see no wrong in the way he had treated James. In fact, he was rather annoyed that he could not have his revenge on the others in James group. If he were very honest with himself, he would admit to the fact that he quite enjoyed the violence and fear that he had inflicted on James. Much too Max annoyance he read in the paper the next morning about the discovery of James body, this really shook him, he had been so confident that he had planned and committed the perfect murder. He had seen the old man with the dog but he did not think the old feller had paid any attention to him. Max needed to rethink his plans for the future. He realised that the police once they discovered the identity of the body would naturally be looking for him in connection with James's death. He did not really think that police would be able to trace him to where he was now. He needed to make sure that he took no chances. Should he move on, should he sit tight? Max sat in deep thought for the rest of the next two days. He finally came up with what he considered the best possible solution. His reasoning went along lines that the best place to hide a person or object was right in front of the people who were searching for it. The best place for him to hide was in prison. He needed to be safely locked away, until the police decided that he could not be found. Once again Max gave his notice to his current landlady he changed hair and beard colour and eyebrows, changed his style of clothing removed the inserts from inside his shoes and found himself a new set of rooms. Max continued to follow the case in the newspaper and soon his name and the case against James appeared in the paper. It was announced in the papers that police were hunting a Mr Kenneth Follet in connection with James murder. They did mention that they would be looking into James's past to find a reason for the brutal act. Max decided it was time for him to establish another new life. He knew that the police had no way to find him. He had spent the last six years doing casual work in restaurants, cafes, in fact any manual job that paid cash-in-hand with no questions. In those six years, he had changed his accommodation every few months; he had always given one month's notice, and never left owing money so that they held nothing against him. Now he stocked up well with food and then spent the next three weeks in his room. His hair and beard became scruffier and unkempt he stopped washing and wore the same clothes day-in day-out even sleeping in them. At the end of the third week, he left his room and dropped an envelope into the landladies, containing enough cash to cover the price to his room for the next six months. He threw most of his belongings into a nearby skip and spent the next week roughing it on the streets begging for money and sleeping in shop doorways. He now looked the part that he had decided that he would play, a fully-fledged Tramp.

In that week he became a regular in s seedy run-down backstreet public Tavern he never had more than a few drinks each evening as he only spend the money that he had been able to beg during the day. He just sat there watching the pub life carry on around him. One evening he watched two young girls walk into the bar and he found it amusing when two older men, men who were old enough to be their fathers tried to chat them up. Two young lads at the bar were also watching the girls. The girls got slightly drunk on the free drinks that the two men were buying them. The two young men stepped in and succeeded in chatting up the girls enough for them to leave the pub together. All the times that he had been in the pub Max had come across as a little bit aggressive not enough to get him thrown out but always enough to make him remembered. At the end of the first week, the regulars had learned to stay clear of that dirty aggressive little tramp. The two men who had lost the girls after spending so much money were not very happy, this state of mind got worst when they realise that the dirty tramp was looking at them and laughing. One of the men looked at Max and said

"Hey dog's breath, what you think you're laughing at?" Max's answer made the whole room go quiet.

"What am I laughing at? I will tell you. I am laughing at two pathetic old men who thought that by buying a couple of young teenage girls are a few cheap drinks they would get their end away. You two idiots got conned, those four Kids were talking outside as I came in, they planned it all you stupid arseholes." One of the men sprang towards Max

"I'll teach you to laugh at me you fucking arsehole." Max had been waiting for this to happen, this was just what he wanted as the man reached out to hit him, Max struck him across the side of the head with his pint pot. The man dropped like a stone. When the man did not get up somebody phoned for an ambulance and the police. Two of the customers held Max until the police got there. Max spent the night locked up. The next morning, the police told him that the man he had hit was now dead. This was not how Max had planned it. He had needed to be in prison, but only for a few months, a charge of GBH should have done that quite nicely. Now the man was dead Max was looking at a charge of manslaughter and he could end up in jail for between 2 and 5 years. This was not what he had planned at all.

Chapter 5

MAX FOUND PRISON LIFE very interesting, and compared to his lifestyle that he had lived for the last six years he found it quite comfortable. For the first time since the death of his grandchildren, Max felt the beginning of life stirring in his blood. It was as if a great weight had been taken away from his mind allowing him a little piece. Although Max's mind was still in a terribly mixed up state, he was beginning to feel that he had discharged some of his debt to his grandchildren. He now wanted to live but he had not yet decided how he would live. He did know that he would never be able to go back and live a normal working person's life. He knew that however, he was going to live, violence would have to be a main part of it.

It did not take Max long to discover that there were four types of people in jail or five if you counted the wardens. The first were people who made their living by being criminals. They took being caught by the law as just another part of the job, they seem to have the attitude that you win some and you lose some. This was a strange way of thinking and Max could not understand it. Maybe this was one way of handling imprisonment for long periods. These people made a very good living out of being criminals and they appeared to be quite clever in their own field of expertise but were a little bit lacking in organisation and self-discipline along with rational thought. The second type of people were like Max was supposed to be, they weren't professional criminals they had done something silly either out of stupidity or drunkenness or they'd done something impulsively. These were people, that should have known better, and to Max way of thinking were not the type of people to bother about. The third type was the ones who were innocent or they claimed to be anyway. These people usually petty criminals' thieves drug peddlers, burglar's muggers in fact they were the riff raff, the scum of the earth. They would rob an old-age pensioner for a few pounds and then accuse everybody of grassing them up. They would never admit that they done anything wrong, they had been fitted up. To Max's way of thinking, they were nothing but minor wingers. They had no commitment to what they did and they had no pride in the crimes that they committed. In fact, they had no pride at all. They would always be a liability to dedicated criminals, as they would turn information over to the police just to make their own lives easier. The fourth type was business people, people who had quite coldly and simply turned to crime. They had done it with the cold calculation and a lot of planning that was common to people running a business. These people had usually only committed one or possibly two big crimes. They had seen a good opportunity to break the law and get away with it making some nice easy money. At the same time the very fact that they might have to hurt somebody to cover, their tracks did not really bother them. Being that they were in prison showed that they had made mistakes and had not quite managed to pull it off. Some of them even though being very close to being arrested had used all sorts of tricks and violence to escape justice. These people really interested Max they were quite honest about what they had done and where they went wrong and they showed no signs of regretting anything that they had tried to do to throw the police of their trail. This group were quite a cold hard-nosed bunch of people, the sort of people that Max could use for an idea that was beginning to take shape in his mind. Max spent the four months that he was in remand studying the different types of people. He decided that the second and third types of inmates were not really worth paying any attention to, it was the other two, the lifetime criminal and the cold professional they gave Max the beginnings of a way of making quite a lot of money.

Chapter 6

AFTER THE DEATH OF James Max had decided that, the best place for him to hide himself away would be in jail. Once you have dropped out of society and live with just cash alone leaving no paper trail, being in jail was not a very hard thing to do. Max had deliberately started a fight, he thought he would get a few weeks in jail for GBH and that was a very good hiding place. Unfortunately, things had gone wrong for Max. The man that Max hit must have had a weak heart, he had died and Max was charged with manslaughter, the judge had been quite understanding, Max was a man living rough who had had a few pints of beer, managed to get into a fight and his opponent had died. Max had received a two-year jail sentence. This had not gone the way Max had planned it but he was just going to have to live with it.

Max spent a lot of time thinking about his future he had soon came to understand that chasing kiddie fiddlers would eventually give him a really long jail sentence and that would get him nowhere. In a way Max was quite honest with himself, he realise that what he had done to James Sindel had not only affected his mind but it had affected or was going to affect his future life. He had decided that violence was a way of life, but if you indulged in violence, you needed to be capable of going all the way. You could have no limits, if somebody had to be seriously hurt or even killed to prove a point then that is what had to be. That bit was easy to work out, what he had to work out next was how he could use the violence to earn him a good living. Max had come to a stage in his life where he was tired of living in cheap lodgings, being dirty and having no real money to splash around. He had decided that when he left jail he would change his life. It did not matter what he had to do, he would have money, lots of money and lots of power. Crime appeared to Max, that if done properly it could be very profitable. To his way of thinking, the best way to make money was from other criminals, he would need three things to make money. First, total ruthlessness, second the ability to organise people and thirdly the power to put total fear and dread it into the sole of your associates and victims.

In the first few months of his sentence Max, carefully and methodically worked out the details of what he was going to do. He would have to get a small gang together, but to make his scheme work properly he could not call it a gang he needed a name for it. He spent a fair bit of time in the library reading about the Mafia he considered; they had the right idea, a few people at the top of the food chain and a very strict code of silence. After a while, he came up with the idea of starting a Guild, calling it a gang or the firm was too much like the movies and he needed it to be very different from anything else any one had ever done before. Once Max left prison he wanted to start big, it was in his mind to takeover most of the criminal activities in a medium-size city.

It took Max a lot of thought and time to work out the details of his new venture. He was very loath to write anything down, after all this prison was full of thieves. The rules of the Guild had to be simple and very straightforward. What he would need is some sort of symbol so that Guild members could recognise each other in the future; he did not want a funny handshake, it had to be some thing nice and simple. Max was stuck for quite a while. The symbol had to be right, he did not want anything that had to be carried like a pin or a token or badge that could be shown. Then one day watching one of the inmates tattooing one of the other prisoners Max had an idea. A small tattoo that would conceal easily and at the same time could be very simple to identify the wearer as a member of the Guild. If he were going to use a tattoo as the identification mark Max decided it had to be something simple, an elaborate tattoo would need a proper tattooist who would be likely to remember it. What he needed was a symbol that was simple enough for one man to tattoo on another man's body without having the skill or equipment, tattooist. Max was at a loss as to what sort of symbol to use. He even tried going through a pack of playing cards looking for some sort of inspiration, but he could find nothing. He did think of using a heart even using a black heart but there was no way that he could believe that that sort to sign would ever be taken seriously, and the last thing that he wanted was for any member of the Guild to be laughed at. One night as he was going over the structure of the Guild the sign for the Guild sprang into his mind. Three Grand Masters would control the Guild. The sign that he would use would be the N°. Three, it was as simple as that. Making it even easier the number 3 tattooed on the back of the left wrist of each member, small enough so that the owner's wristwatch would cover it. Simply pushing the wristwatch back the identified the wearer to any other member. There were plenty of people in the prison and elsewhere capable of making that type of tattoo for a very small price, done if needed with a pot of black ink and a sharp needle, not the type of tattoo to stand out in other people's minds. Now that he had this sorted, he set about working out the rules and conditions of membership to the Guild. He wanted it so that he could make a good living but he was also aware that he would not be capable of taking all the profits and running the Guild buy himself. He would need to have at least two more partners they would be the Grand Masters. Next in line after the three Grand Masters would come three maybe four Sub Masters they would be like the lieutenants, each would be in charge of a separate part of the organisation. Each member would pay an entry fee of £5,000 plus five per cent of all their criminal earnings that were committed in the name of the Guild or crimes sanctioned by the Guild. Part of the entrance initiation would have to be an act of such magnitude that there could be no going back on the Guild without the permission of the Guild. Max came up with the idea that each new member would have to commit murder in front of other members of the Guild and that murder would have to be videoed so that it could be held against the new member if required. That way no member of the Guild would find it beneficial to give the authorities any sort of information concerning the business of the Guild. The Guild would consist of three men, himself and two others they would be known as the Grand Masters. Each of the Grandmasters would kill a man or woman in the presence of at least one of the other two, the killings would be on video if possible. That would make each of if three Grandmasters beholden to the other two. As each Grand Master introduced a member that Grandmaster would be present when the new member committed his murder to gain entrance to the Guild. Each new member could then introduce other new members; each of these new members had to kill somebody in the presence of the member that introduced them and one Grandmaster or Sub Master. Max reasoned that the police or any other agency could not penetrate the Guild because a witnessed murder was a price that was too hard and too high for any police force in this country to pay. Any member of the Guild could put forward the plans for any crime that they wished to commit, to the Grandmasters for approval. If the Guild refused to sanction the crime, then the members would not be covered or protected under the terms of the Guild. The Guild would for a reasonable price provide specialised equipment if necessary, also any crime that they committed that was sanctioned by the Guild would mean that they would give up five per cent of their gross takings of that crime. That split in halves, one-half set-aside into a fund that insured members an income whilst in jail, as long as he was on Guild business. Each member at the time of his trial could select one person to receive that money as either a lump sum or a monthly payment. The other half split between the three Grandmasters. The Guild would take on various assignments from outside groups such as assassinations and possibly in house corrections, also outside organisations could hire Guild specialists such as safe crackers alarm specialists and even body guards, for that the outsiders would be charged a fee plus 15 per cent of net profit made by the crime. Max reasoned that once the Guild got started the Guild would make a considerable amount of money, and naturally, the Grand Masters would take the lion's share. Max thought that he had worked out a way e of running a criminal group with very few chances of anybody infiltrating it. He could see no reason for any member to give evidence against them because of the videos held on each person, any outsider that gave evidence against them would have be dealt with in such a way that no one else would ever think of going against the Guild. The way Max had tried to work out the basics of the Guild meant that if any agency tried to infiltrate the Guild with an undercover operator they would automatically put that person in a position where to carry out their mission they would have to commit a murder. The way he had it worked out it should not be possible to fake the murder. There was no way that any court in this country could excuse the cold-blooded murder of any body even the worse criminal going, just to get a conviction against another criminal. Because that murder filmed and witnessed by the very people that the agents were trying to infiltrate, there was no way that it was possible to bluff the entrance initiation. Now all Max had to do was to find two Grandmasters.

Chapter 7

THE TWO GRANDMASTERS THAT Max needed had to be chosen with a lot of care and attention to their abilities. He needed two entirely different types of people. One of them needed to be hard, ruthless, without fear and totally without thought to anybody else's feelings. That person would be his main muscle man. This man would be the person that he would be relying on to keep everything in order as far as collecting money and punishments were concerned. This man had to be very loyal to the Guild. The second Grandmaster needed to be just as ruthless as Max and the other Grandmaster but be able to give the impression that he was really quite a respectable person. He needed to be a businessperson that could look after the accounts of the Guild and the interest that the Guilds money would accumulate. As the Guild would only deal in hard cash that cash needed investing, after all they could not just put it under their mattresses. These two men needed to be men that he could trust, men that would not panic or flap when something started to go wrong. These two men along with him if things went well would end up grasping an entire city in a steel fist, for this was Max's aim he intended to takeover and control the crime in a medium-sized city. Max had decided that the Grandmasters, Sub Masters and members would be mainly men. He was not being a sexist and he was not under the silly idea that women were the weakest sex; he needed the brutal strength of men. Of course, in a male prison there was not a chance to get anybody but men as members because he still had a fair while to go on his sentence. Apart from that, he had never come across a true woman criminal. He could take his time picking his two Grandmasters.

Max had masqueraded as a down-and-out dirty scruffy looking man for so long. Since being sentenced, he had managed to keep dyeing his hair and beard brown he revelled in the ability to have a shower near enough when he wanted one. He was in the shower unit one-day when in walked a man called Jake. Jake was one of the real hard men and he was currently serving four years for assault with a deadly weapon. Jakes only name was Jake he never gave any other name but Jake. He was a large man, very strong and also very quick to anger. He had followed the style of many hard men by shaving his head but leaving a small goatee beard on his chin. He had served quite a lot of time in prison, mainly short sentences. This one, of four years was the longest one he had served, he had spent his life as hired muscle for different people, he had tried a few things by himself and each time he tried, he got it wrong and ended up in prison again. Jake was not very thick he just was not very well organised; unfortunately he had more control over his muscles than he did over his brain.

Max was the only person in the shower unit, and Jake ignored Max apart from a slight nod of his head, they had not said more than a few words to each other since Max arrived at the prison. Suddenly four men appeared in the shower room door,

"You fucking bastard you're for it now," one of the men screamed. With that, they piled through the door and headed straight towards Jake, backing him into a corner of the shower unit. Max saw that they all had a weapon of some sort. Three of them had clubs made from bits that they had stolen from the prison workshop, while the fourth one carried a homemade knife. The knife made from a razor blade and a toothbrush; it was a simple but effective way to make a weapon. You simply melt the bristles of the brush with a lighter and while they are still molten insert the blade and hold it in place until the bristles harden. This was the sort of situation that Jake was quite at home with, these types of people were no threat to him really, he had handled six or seven at a time in the past. Instead of wasting his time, trying to talk to the four men, Jake set his head down into his shoulders and took one pace forward, his left fist shot out and one man went down. Max was fascinated although he now knew that he enjoyed inflicting violence. This was the first time he had seen a real no holds barred scrap. The bloke with the knife and one of the remaining clubmen still faced off to Jake, already the knifeman had managed to draw blood across Jakes chess and along one of his forearms. The fourth man turned to Max and raised his club. Although Max had nothing to do with this set to it looked as if Max was going to take a beating. That way there would be no witnesses, it was clear to Max that he and Jake were about to die. Max didn't hesitate, as the club started to rise he lashed out with his right foot and kicked the man straight between his legs, of course Max was barefoot and it felt as if his big toe and possibly the one next to it might have broken. At the same time, he felt the man's testicles squash in a sickening crunch that made his attacker scream out with pain and vomit straight on the floor. As the man crumpled into a heap on the floor, rolling about clutching his private parts, he rolled into the legs of the man with the knife. This gave Jake all the edge that he needed, he lashed out with his fist and doubled the knife man over with a massive blow to the pit of his stomach, as he bent double, Max picked up a club from one of the fallen men and swung it round house-style. It landed across the back of the knife man's head. The man died immediately, meanwhile Jake swung one of his massive fists and the fourth and final man collapsed against the shower wall. Max decided that now was the time to take charge of the situation. He looked at Jake and said,

"You know they intended to kill you? This really has nothing to do with me but they were going to kill me as well, just because I was here, that would leave no witnesses." Jake was having trouble trying to understand why somebody would help him for no reason, then he slowly started to understand what Max had said, a grin came over his face,

"I owe you a big one, Max, that is your name isn't it?" Max nodded

"I have killed this one and apart from killing the other three we could be in trouble." Jake pondered over this for a little while and then came up with the idea.

"The other three will talk, plus we will spend the rest of our time looking over our shoulders waiting for them to get revenge on us." Max realised that Jake was having trouble with the thinking so he said,

"Best we top the other three as well." A real big smile came to Jakes face,

"No witnesses!" he said.

"So it's just you and I Max?" Max held out his hand and said,

"I've done one; let's make it two each, that way we don't have to worry about each other." Jake did not have the quickest brain in the world, but this bit he understood straightaway, if they both killed two men, neither of them would ever have to worry about the other one grassing on him. To Jakes, way of thinking this was an ideal situation. Without any more to do, Jake promptly lifted one of the unconscious men to a sitting position and taking him under the chin with one hand he wrapped his other arm round the man shoulders, the sharp pull on each of his arms produced a real loud crack as the man's neck snapped. Max picked up the homemade knife from the floor and placed it in the hand of the original knifeman then moved the man's arm so that he could guide the knife across the third blokes throat, the blood spurted into the air drenching Jake and Max. Jake just laughed and turning to the last living assailant, he lashed out with his heel catching the man square on the side of his jaw breaking his neck, as he lay unconscious. Max and Jake quickly stepped into the shower to wash the blood away.

The two cuts on Jake turned out to be quite deep and they really needed stitching. Max and Jake dried themselves off and walked back to Jakes cell as if nothing had happened. Inside Jakes cell, he produced a large darning needle and some thread.

"You will need to stitch me up Max there's no way that I can go to the Infirmary, we really need to keep this quiet." Jake laid on his bunk and Max set to with the needle and thread, all credit to Jake not once did he cry out as the needle and thread pulled his open fresh wound together. Max hoped that the wardens believed that the four men had had a falling-out and managed to kill each other. It was set up and very badly put together, and nearly impossible to believe. That the wardens would want as little fuss as possible was their best hope. Max believed that he had found his first Grandmaster.

Over the next few weeks Max and Jake became quite firm friends mainly because Max cultivated the man as best as he could. They now had a bond between them that would last them the rest of their lives. Over a period of time Jake told Max about his life, how we had done five short prison terms before this one in the last 25 years. Jake actually admitted that most of the times he was arrested, was for the silliest of reasons. Like he said he did not have the ability to plan things properly, he always managed to miss out one detail or another that landed him back in jail. Max gradually put the idea of the Guild to Jake explaining that Jake would not have to put up money or pay a fee, as being one of the three Grandmasters it was them that were going to make the profit. For once in his life Jake did not jump in without thinking, he took his time thinking things over. After a few days he came to Max and asked,

"Being a Grandmaster in this Guild of yours is a good idea it could be a way for me to stay out of prison. You must have worked out by now that I am just muscle not a bloody leader of men, and I am no good at bloody paperwork, in fact I can only just about read and write." Max laughed, by this time he and Jake were firm friends, so they could have a laugh and joke and be quite honest with each other, after they had killed two men each they were committed to each other. This gave Jake the confidence to feel that maybe he was on an equal footing with a man who was far more intelligent than he was.

"Jake you excel at violence you are going to be the Guilds Mr muscle man and as long as you can follow orders then let me look after the money and the leadership's side, I will keep you in money if you can keep the Guild members in line. I will also do my level best to keep you and them out of prison." A large grin appeared on Jakes face,

"That's what I thought you wanted me for. No way could I see you using me for my brain power." He then rolled up his left sleeve, pulled back his watch and showed Max a small black number three tattooed on his left wrist.

"Count me in Max; I've never done any good by myself so I may as well throw in my lot with you."

So began the most violent time in the history of that medium-size city from the small beginnings of Max and Jake joining forces to form one of the hardest to penetrate groups of heartless violent killers anyone could imagine. They would be known as, The 3. Max and Jake now had to find a third Grandmaster, considering different people for different reasons; they would have to make the right choice of the third member of their group.

Chapter 8

ADAM DAVIES SAT IN his office he was fed up; a lot of time had passed since the grotesque remains of James Sindel had been found. From the bits and pieces that had been salvaged from the fire and from the prison records the name belonging to the body was soon found. Adam was surprised at first by the medical report from the prison it seemed as if Mr J Sindel was rather accident-prone. In six years he had to be taken to the Infirmary 46 times with all sorts of injuries, it was only when he read the report of James trial that Adam began to understand the reason behind all the damage that James had suffered in prison. Adam being a homosexual understood what it was like to be different from the rest of humankind; he had over the years undergone a few bad moments caused by people with no tolerance for his sort. Adam was willing to let people lead their own lives, but even he could not tolerate kiddie fiddlers. Reading the reports on James Sindel, Adam came to the belief that Ken Follet was the likely suspect. It stood to reason, the man had lost his grandchildren, his daughter was now no more than a vegetable and there had been an incident in the courtroom when Follet had threatened to kill Sindel at the earliest opportunity. James Sindel released at 8 am and was dead by 7 pm that same day. It was not rocket science that was needed, to work out the case against Follet. Everything was so open and shut that in a few hours Follet would be inside and the team would be down the pub having a few drinks. Adam sighed, after that it had all gone wrong. Ken Follet, his address was on the files; the police dispatched to arrest him, only to find that he had sold the house six years previously. That was only a minor hiccup. Ken's National

Insurance number broadcast across the Internet. Working or signing on the National Insurance number would show up his whereabouts, OK it would take time but he it would turn up. Nothing, not even a few days' work showed up on any computer. Adam could not understand it. Kenneth Follet was a normal honest working-class sort of bloke with not even a parking ticket to his name. A man that was in fact squeaky clean, how could he just vanish like a puff of smoke? This sort of thing was to be expected, from a lifelong criminal, not from a man like Ken.

Next all banks were contacted and just at first the banks acted as banks act, they offered nothing, then one of the young CID men managed to wheedle out of a female cashier that in fact her bank did hold an account in the name of Ken Follet. There was money in it, there was no way she would tell him how much but it had remained unused for the last six years. Apparently, it was some sort of trust set up to support his daughter if she ever made a recovery. There was just no trace of Kenneth Follet. His photo posted around the police stations, again nothing. Adam now believed that it might be possible that Ken Follet had left the country. In a way he was glad, he thought that Ken deserved a break but he did wonder if Ken had managed to slip back into the country in time to kill Sindel. Adam had already taken a lot of dissension from the press, but that was fading as other news of crimes came in. Adam had decided that this case was more than likely to end up as being unsolved. Maybe one day he would get lucky.

Chapter 9

AFTER LOOKING AT A lot of different prisoners Max and Jake decided that the man they wanted was Robert King, Rab, as he liked to be called. Rab was a rank loner, 6 ft tall, he was a Glaswegian man and although very thin he had the wiry strength of a man twice his weight, there was very little fat on him even though he did not do a lot of exercise. He had a slightly hooked nose that made him look like a hawk about to swoop on its prey. The dark brown eyes seemed capable of looking inside your very soul. Rab was a complete and utterly ruthless man; he had no compassion for anyone or anything it would appear that all the years of dealing with figures had left him cold and calculating. He had been a fully trained accountant and at a young age had his own small firm with a good client list, most of the shady businesses in Glasgow used Rabs firm. Nobody knew why but in a very cold calculating way, he decided that the money his clients were stashing away should really be his. He considered that over the years, he had saved them millions of pounds in tax; it was time that he should receive the luxuries that they were getting from his hard work and knowledge. Rab had always believed that to be successful in business you must be bold and daring and that is exactly what he became, bold and daring, over a period of two weeks he managed to stash away four million pounds from a total of 16 of his clients. Up until then Rab had been a fairly quiet peaceful person although very resourceful when it came to manipulating the tax rules and regulations. When the net started to close in on him Rab suddenly found he had a violent streak that he had not realised that he had. He could see that he was about to be caught, apparently people did not like losing a lot of money. Bold and daring being his new watchwords Rab killed two of the clients that he had robbed mainly to stop them giving evidence against him but also to frighten the others into keeping quiet. He beat one of the female clients so badly that she was in hospital for nearly three months and it was touch-and-go whether she would survive; even then, she remained in a wheelchair until she died 12 years later. When the police arrived to arrest him, he put up such as struggle that four police officers ended up in hospital. Rab badly beaten by the police and he was not fit to be put before the magistrate for over a fortnight. Unfortunately, for him the police managed to find quite a lot for the money that Rab had stashed away. At his trial, the judge said that he had misused and abused the trust that his clients had invested in him. The judge then kindly awarded Rab 15 years. Rab had not been a model prisoner over the course of the years. He did not receive parole in fact he had time added to his sentence. When Max met him, he had already served 18 years and still had a couple more to go. In the years, that Rab had been in prison the wardens and other inmates had come to realise that Rab was a very dangerous loner, if left to himself he was easy to handle, but rubbed the wrong way and his character would change in a split second. Rab prowled the landings and rest rooms of the prison like a wounded lion there were days when the wardens that knew him and recognised the look in his eyes would walk around him, and kept out of his way. A few years before, he got upset when one of the inmates called him a Scot's git. Rab was reading a newspaper in the rest room area, next to a group of prisoners, they were laughing and joking just chatting, chilling out telling a few jokes. One of the man a little opportunist burglar and low-life criminal that nobody really liked had just finished telling the rather tall story about breaking into a house, finding a lot for a very expensive jewellery and then discovering the owner's wife in bed naked. He went on to tell how she had opened her legs for him to help himself in the hope that he would not take her jewellery. According to him, he was such a good lover that after screwing her at least five times, she gave him the jewellery anyway. That was when Rab snorted in disgust; the storyteller turned round and said

"Something wrong you fucking Scots git?" Rab did not hesitate he picked up a tin plate that was on the table and struck the man across the face with the edge of it. In doing so, he broke the man's nose and blinded him in the left eye, by the time the wardens had pulled, him off he had further managed to break three of the man's ribs and his right collarbone.

Max and Jake spent the next few months gradually getting to know Rab, it was a slow process because the man was not ready to trust anybody, he was really a hundred per cent loner who liked his own company and he had little trust in anybody bar himself. Gradually the three of them became friends and it turned out that Rab, once you got to know him and got through his hard exterior was quite a character. Most of the money that he had stolen had been recovered, it turned out that he had very little stashed away for later. However with Rabs knowledge of accountancy, Jakes ability for real hard violent attacks and Max's planning capability it looked as if these three men would form one formidable group as the Grandmasters of the Guild. Once the principles were explained to him he thought to over, and very quickly his sharp mind soon sorted out the advantage of their scheme, he agreed to join. Rab needed a victim to kill to complete his entrance to the Guild. Max and Jake could not video him killing somebody, in the prison, nobody had a video of them doing their deed. Rab could pick his own victim. Of course, the killing could not be done with a gun, the authorities were not too happy with prisoner's running about with guns.

The man that Rab chose was a little skinny man he had been in prison for about 10 years and for the last few years had been a red band, it was a known fact that he liked young boys; also, most inmates believed that he was an informant. It was best that he would do it at the evening free time, when cells were open. Giving the inmates the freedom to mingle from cell to cell or just rest. The three of them watched and waited until the man went back to his cell for some tobacco. Once he was inside, they quickly stepped in and shut the door behind them. As the man turned, round to see what was happening Rab stepped forward and bringing his right hand up very quickly he struck the man on the point of his chin with the heel of his hand the man's head snapped back striking in the wall of the cell with a sickening dull thud. As the man slid to the floor, he left a trail of blood down the wall tiles. As Rab bent over the now unconscious man, he pulled from his pocket his toothbrush with an open razor blade taped to the handle. Pulling the man's head back by his hair Rab coldly and calmly without hurry opened the man's throat from one side of his neck to the other, as soon as the blood started to flow fast Rab pulled the man's head forward to stop the blood spraying all over the cell. Rab rinsed his hands and the toothbrush in the sink; the three men shut the cell door behind them and casually walked back to Rabs cell. In his cell Rab carefully removed the razor blade from the toothbrush washing them both, then he replace the blade in his razor and everything was back to normal. The next day a black number three-shaped tattoo appeared on the back of Rabs left wrist, now there were three members to the Guild.

There were now three of them to start looking for prospective members, unfortunately, the only people they could consider now were already in prison and these men did not have the membership-joining price, or were not in the position where they could lay their hands on it, but also there was the joining initiation. At best, a prison is a hard violent place to live in; it is not easy to pick out lots of people that need killing to prove a man's worthiness of joining the Guild. Also in the prison, there was not a lot of call for people to pay to have a criminal act committed, so although the principles were good the business of the Guild was put on hold until the Grandmasters were free.

Chapter 10

MAX WAS THE FIRST one to be released from prison, he was now about to embark on an entirely new way of life. This life was going to embrace violence and crime, up until the death of his grandchildren Max had given the impression that he was a nice everyday family man, an honest citizen; he had been a pillar of the community. That he now realise got him nowhere, everything had been taken away from him that he held precious, in the last few years the only thing that had given him any sort of satisfaction had been the violence concerning the death of James. To his now twisted mind if violence could give enjoyment and added to that enough money to give him a good lifestyle, and if turning to crime met those needs, then that was what he was going to do. Now that he was out of prison, he needed to find some recruits for the Guild. Now the Guild consisted just three Grandmasters, what he needed was normal members to the Guild to start bringing in an income, with no members then he and the other two Grandmasters would make no money. To Max this was a simple statement of fact. Rectifying this would mean that people would die and other people would be used, but this did not bother Max in the slightest. So far, Max had killed James, the middle-aged man in the pub and the 2 inmates in prison. He had been present at the death of the man that Rab had killed and at the deaths of the two men, which Jake killed in the shower room. To be truthful he found that he had really enjoyed it; the power rush was fantastic he wanted to do this again but this time he wanted to make money doing it. After all, why could he not earn money doing what he liked? Jake, was next to be released from prison, and until that time; Max was going to get recruits ready to join the Guild. Although Max was violent and quite capable of planning, events he had to admit that he needed Jake to use his street knowledge to help pick the right people as recruits for the Guild.

While in prison, Max had selected the medium-size city that the Guild would takeover. It was Max's job to lay the ground roots for the Guild. He had done his full term in prison so he had no probation officer to worry about he was entirely by himself. First things first he went to one of the bank's that he had money deposited in and drew out some spending money. He then went and found himself some lodgings in a rough part of the city. He stayed in the lodgings for the next month while he got used to finding his way around the city. He mapped the city out into roughly three areas firstly there was the real posh area, secondly there was a nice quieter area with supermarkets and reasonably clean looking houses and thirdly there was a rough part. That rough part if it had been in a Cowboy and Indian film would have been the red light district, to say that it was rough was putting it rather mildly even the police would only enter that part of town in pairs. This rough area was what Max was interested in, there was more crime in this small patch in one-day them most cities had in a month. Once he got to know the city Max went out shopping and bought himself some really nice respectable clothes he then went to an hairdresser and had his beard trimmed right down to a goatee style beard and his hair trimmed down so that it was fairly short, Max now gave the appearance of being quite a smart gentleman. Then he went to the quieter area of the city and found some lodgings in quite a large boarding house with a very respectable proprietor. He now had a base that was well away from where he and his companions intended to earn their money.

While he was getting to know the city, Max had used many of the backstreet grotty little public houses. He was now on nodding terms with quite a few barmaids and even a few of the customers, to form a pattern to his existence Max had been going to the same pubs at roughly the same times throughout the days and evenings. He never really engaged any one in conversation he had just sat quiet watching people's behaviour. He was looking for people that were hard and ruthless, he needed people who were used to extreme violence and people that had come to realise that the power that they held could really control other people's lives with fear and terror. Max thought there was no way that he was going to a recruit very many members by himself. Until Jakes release from prison, he would try to recruit a couple to make the beginnings of a fighting fund for when things really got going. The only problem that he could see was there would be a sudden increase in murders in one local area, not so much a problem in this rough area, they would have to cross that bridge when they started recruiting in larger numbers.

When Max first thought of creating a Guild off violent people he had envisioned it being all men. Max had been leading a normal average life and he was old-fashioned enough to believe that women were capable of showing great strength and determination but they were on average nice gentle souls that although they had sharp tongues they were soft gentle creatures that looked after the children. Therefore, it came as a great surprise to him that the first person he considered as a new recruit was in fact a woman. Sally Ann Watson, when he first saw her she was sitting at a table in a dingy little public bar in the backstreets of the city, Max had been in the bar for 20 minutes before he even noticed her. By no one standards could she be called a pretty woman, standing about five foot six inches in her stocking feet more muscular than fat she had a reasonable looking body for a 40 year-old woman. Although the area was rough her clothes were extremely good quality, nothing flashy with bright posh labels, just very good quality and expensive. Her face was a real letdown, the skin under her make-up looked nice and the make-up, was put on with a great deal of skill but not all the make-up in the world could hide the harshness of her features. This woman had been round the block a few times. With her cold sharp features and a slightly oversize nose, a generous mouth showing good well looked after teeth and ice cold dark green eyes she gave the impression that to argue with her was about as profitable as arguing with a solid brick wall. At first glance, she fitted in very well with this type a bar. Max watched Sally for over a week before he was aware of what she did for a living and then he only found out by accident. Sally sat at the same table in the bar every evening just after nine until closing time slowly sipping pints of beer. After watching her for her for a lot of time Max could see that, she only drank two pints of beer each night although she gave the impression of a heavy drinker. She would talk to anybody that wanted to engage her in conversation, which was mainly men and although they talked to her, they always left before her. At first, Max thought she was a prostitute taking a couple of hours off each night. After a while he realise that although she did talk to plenty of people she did not show any friendliness or politeness towards them.

Then he started to notice more about the people that spoke to her, it would appear that the same men came to talk to her at roughly the same time each evening, without being too conspicuous he started to pay closer attention to this woman. Nearly every man that sat down and spoke to her for a while managed to slip something under a table to her that she slipped into her bag, they would then have a brief discussion as the man drank his drink, then he would leave. This was happening three, sometimes four times an evening. One evening Max was in the pub when a man that he had not noticed before came in and started arguing with Sally. Max could not hear what they were saying but by the body language of the man, Max got the impression that Sally could be in a lot of trouble. The argument went on for quite some time and the only words that Max could hear were all swear words surprising enough coming mainly from Sally. All of a sudden Sally got up and walked out of the pub, the man looked round the bar making sure that nobody was paying any attention to him or Sally then he followed her out of the door. Max did not want to get involved; all said and done it was none of his business. He did not really like the idea of a man beating up a woman. After a few moments, Max decided that he would have to go and see what was happening. As he walked out of the door Sally came back into the pub, she did not have one hair out of place and no cuts or bruises. This caused Max a brief moment of worry he thought that maybe Sally had taken the punishment below the neckline of her clothes. Max had only gone a few yards from the pub door when he saw the man crawling out of the entrance to an alley. Max walked over and looked down at the man, what he saw surprised him. The man had taken a severe beating only a few bruises to his face but the way he was trying to crawl did look as if both his knees and his elbows had taken a serious pounding. Max helped the bloke to his feet and lent him against a wall. The man was now holding his ribcage rather tenderly. He looked Max straight in the eyes and said "Thank-you, now Fuck off, this is private." Max asked the man if he was going back in to sort out Sally. "Not fucking likely, that fucking bitch used a knuckle duster on me. But I will fucking well sort her out one way or another." With that, the man stumbled off and Max saw him get into a large car further down the road and drive off.

The more Max had seen of Sally the more he could admire what she had done. The man that had taken a beating was obviously a pimp, and as he thought that, the rest of it dropped into place. The other men they came in and spoke to her were also pimps, and they came in to pay Sally the previous day's takings. She must control most of the prostitutes and pimps in the whole of this area. Max walked back into the pub and ordered another pint, as he put his hand in his pocket for his money a voice behind him said, "I'll pay for that." Max looked at Sally and she grinned, "I haven't heard the police or ambivalence, so I take it that you know when to keep your mouth shut. Why don't we sit down?" Over the next three or four weeks Max started to study Sally carefully. He soon managed to find out that Sally was definitely not on the game. What she was doing was offering protection to about 15 different pimps. Any that failed to do what she told them to do or to pay her a weekly fee were taken to one side and given a slap, to remind them who was boss. The beatings didn't happen very often because Sally made them so harsh that the other pimps stayed in line. Normally when a new pimp started he went a few weeks conforming, then he would decide that he did not need Sally. Sally would then give him a harsh beating. Then he would conform like a good little boy. The beating also served as a good reminder to the rest of the pimps and prostitutes that Sally was in charge. After she had beaten the pimp outside and then bumped into Max as he came out of the door she realised that he would put two and together and work out what had happened. She had sat down at her table and just encase the police had come for her; she had hung her knuckle duster on a hook that she had previously placed under the table. With that evidence out of the way, the police would not believe that a little woman like Sally would have the ability to beat up a man like the pimp. When Max had walked back into the pub and stood at the bar to order a drink Sally was impressed. Through the next few weeks Max and Sally got to be, quite good friends as was his intentions he needed to get close to the people that he wanted to join the Guild. The Guild was going to become his family, one evening he talked to Sally about the Guild.

Max did not offer to let Sally joined the Guild he just wanted her to understand the main principles; he wanted her to ask to join. Sally caught on to the idea very quickly, although she thought it was a good idea she could see no way that it would benefit her. Especially if she had to pay £5,000 to join, plus a percentage of earnings and on top of all that she had to kill somebody and have it witnessed on video well that was something else. Max spent the next few days explaining the advantages of the Guild to Sally. The fact that she would have to kill somebody was no deterrent to her; she just did not like the idea of the witnesses. When he explained that, she could pick the person herself, which meant that she could get rid of somebody who was in competition with her or someone who was causing her grief made a lot of sense to her. In fact, that part to the deal was really quite an attractive proposition to Sally. Max explain that the Guild would be making it worthwhile to Sally as the pimps that she controlled would be used by the Guild without the pimps knowing who controlled them and any profit from their work would go to Sally. The girls used by the Guild would all be ones that fell under the jurisdiction of Sally's pimps. Of course the profit would go to Sally, although as Max said the Guild would require a bit of a discount. As the Guild intended to control all the crime in this city before making more money if Sally joined them Max could see no reason why she could not control all the girls, pimps, peepshows, brothels, massage parlours and any other interest that involved any type of sex act. In fact, Sally could now control the whole sex industry in the City. What Max didn't have to point out to Sally was the fact that if she were to refuse somebody else would be put in charge of the sex industry and that would put Sally on the wrong side of the Guild, now Sally could see the point of the Guild and insisted on joining then and there. Max really wanted to wait until at least one of the other Grandmasters were out and about before he initiated new members. Although Sally was eager to get started, she understood the reason for him wanting.

Max had found his first member.

Chapter 11

BERNARD WAS HAVING A brilliant day. First thing that morning he had had a phone call asking him if he could supply a brand new BMW, preferably in a very dark red or maroon colour. The man that phoned him was willing to pay him an extra £5,000 bonus if Bernard could deliver the car by the end of the day. Bernard had eaten a very good breakfast egg, bacon, mushrooms and black pudding accompanied by two cups of coffee he then had a shave, showered, dressed in a nice smart business suit and left the house thinking that all was well in the world. He caught a bus into the centre of the city; he then walked around for 10 minutes until he could find a car that somebody had been silly enough to leave the keys in the ignition. He eventually found an old Ford Sierra, which he promptly stole. He sat outside the BMW main dealer's for over two hours until he saw a man drive away in a nice maroon BMW that was brand new. The owner had no idea about Bernard following him, as he drove from the city. After a while, the young man drove into the suburbs of the city, where he pulled up outside of a very nice detached house jumping from the car he left the driver's door open, and ran up the steps to the front door and rang a bell. He was obviously going to show off his brand new car Bernard did not hesitate he pulled the Sierra up behind the BMW stepped out of the Sierra walked six paces to the BMW climbed in, shut the driver's door and drove off this was going to be the easiest extra £5,000 he had ever made.

He phoned his contact from a payphone and told the man that he could deliver the car within 20 minutes, his contact wanted to know if he could put it off for a couple of hours as he was in the middle of VAT inspection. This was not a problem to Bernard, he drove the car to a lock-up that he had rented for many years in a false name, parked the car making sure to lock it, he then walked away from the garage and bought himself a newspaper as he went and had lunch in a local cafe that he knew. Bernard was driving the BMW through the city on his way to deliver it, the blue flashing lights in the rear-view mirror made him swear strongly under his breath. There was a lot of money riding on this car and he did not intend to lose it if he could help it. He turned into an empty side street hoping that the police car behind was after somebody else. It looked like his luck was out when the police car turned into the side street behind him. He could try to dodge them, if he did that the car registration and his description would be all over the police radio network, making the car so hot that he would not be able to sell it. Bernard was a professional he knew that it did not matter how good a driver he was, he was not capable of out running radio waves. Like a good citizen, he pulled into the side of the road and switched off the engine. They police officer in the passenger seat of the police car got out and approached the BMW. Bernard watched him in the rear-view mirror and thought to himself,

"This guy looks full of his own piss and importance." The police office wrapped his knuckles on a driver's window; Bernard pressed the button for the electric window and as the glass slid down the police officer started his well rehearsed opening lines.

"Good afternoon sir, are you the owner of this vehicle? If so could I please see your documents?" Bernard sat there looking at the police officer

"What a pillock" he thought,

"No officer I am not the owner of the car as you well know." the police officer now went into his John Wayne mode. He stepped back from the door of the car readied himself for instant action should Bernard try to run for it, and said,

"Get out of the car and spread your legs wide. Place your hands on the roof." Bernard did as he was told, after all he was carrying no weapons or identification in fact all he had in his possession were some notes and some loose change in his right hand pocket and a packet of tissues in his left jacket pocket. He was in no rush he wanted to study the surrounding area he had already worked a plan of action in his mind, and he knew exactly what he was going to do. There was no way that he intended to lose his freedom just because a couple of coppers could read a number plate. There would always be another chance to earn money. The officer that searched had found nothing, and because Bernard had made no attempt at violence or coursed a fuss and because Bernard had admitted that, the car was, stolen. The police officer now made the biggest and final mistake of his very short life. He had decided that

Bernard was an honest crook the sort a crook that once caught put his hands up and came quietly, he decided he could handle Bernard so he did not think it necessary to put the handcuffs on him.

"I need you to accompany me back to the police car sir." Bernard and the officer walked towards a police car.

The police officer gave the thumbs up sign to the driver of the police patrol car, at same time having that silly smile on his face that said what a clever boy I have been, I am very clever. As the police officer and Bernard got into the back seat of the patrol car, the driver turned his head round, and speaking to the officer, he said

"The paperwork for this will take us right into overtime, especially if we do the initial questioning now." They were the last words that that man ever uttered. Bernard's right hand shot out and the heel of his palm struck the driver under the point of his nose forcing the bone in his nose to go upwards into his brain. He was dead before his head hit the dashboard. As the officer fell backwards, Bernard elbowed the other officer in the throat. Then turning quickly so that he was facing the side of the officer, his hand shot out this time his fist was clenched all bar the knuckle of his index finger, which was pushed forward, he struck the offices temple and for the second time in as many seconds, a man died. He had made sure to touch nothing as he got into the car and he made sure to touch nothing as he got out. Bernard then walked casually back to the BMW as if the police had finished with him. When he got back into the BMW, he was angry; this car was worth a lot of money to him plus the £5,000 bonus also his buyer was waiting for it. Now he would have to get rid of it that meant either losing the Sale or stealing another one. Bernard was a careful man he liked things worked out well before he actually committed himself to any action. He had even planed what he would do if the police ever stopped him, and today he had done exactly what he had planned. Obviously, the police had been on the alert after the theft of the brand-new BMW if he tried to steal another one-today day he would really be pushing his luck a little too far. He had kept a clean charge sheet all these years by keeping things simple and although it hurt his pride and his pocket, he would have to lose this sale. Bernard left the scene of the crime and drove around for 10 minutes, just to clear his thoughts, after all anything done in haste or without planning usually went wrong. He pulled the car into a side street just past a service station. Taking off his jacket and tie, he undid his shirt to the waist rolled up his sleeves. Then ruffled his hair and from his jacket pocket he took a handful of the tissues which he rolled up and put in either side of his mouth this gave him a totally different look. He was now a scruffy looking man with a fat face. He walked back to the service station and bought a packet of cigarettes, a box of matches and a plastic petrol can, which he filled with two gallons of petrol.

He then drove the BMW around until he found a quiet side road with an alley leading between two houses. He drove to the end of a road turned a corner and parked the car. He then walked back to the alley. He walked along the passageway and found that it came out two streets away. He went back to the BMW and drove round the block until he was back opposite the alley. Very quickly, he opened all the windows about an inch. Emptied the petrol over the inside of the car then set the petrol can on the front seat. He stood outside the car and lit one of cigarettes, the rest he threw into the car he then opened the matchbox exposing all the live heads. Breaking most of the cigarette off from the tip he them pushed the cigarette into the matchbox, until the lit end was close to the match heads, partially closed the box. The burning cigarette end was now about an eighth of an inch an inch away from the live heads. He them placed matchbox on the front seat of the car. As he walked up the alley, he spat out the tissue from his mouth and put them in his pocket. The end of the cigarette went into his pocket also. He quickly put on his tie, rolled down his shirt sleeves and replaced his jacket he was combing his hair with his fingers as he walked out of the alley a totally different looking man from the one that walked away from the BMW. Within a few moments, there was a sudden dull thump type of noise and he could see billing smoke rise in the air, the petrol helped by the good airflow would remove any traces of his fingerprints or DNA that he might have been careless and left behind. He now knew that there was no evidence in the BMW to connect him to the car theft or the deaths of the police officers. The events that had happened could not be helped it was just the luck of the draw that a police car had come up behind him and that the police officer had recognised the car from their stolen list. Bernard had just killed two police officers rather than get arrested, for stealing a car, he felt no remorse about this and in fact, it had made no Impact on him at all. Bernard had been cared for in an orphanage, after his mother had dumped him at a hospital. He had had a very hard life and it was not a very happy one. Once he could drive, he had started stealing cars, not for joyriding like the other kids but as a business. The police had never actually caught Bernard, mainly because he thought things through very quickly and was a very capable planner when it came to escape routes. He knew this city like the back of his hand. At any time that he was in a car that was not a hundred per cent kosher, then before he drove it away in his mind he had not only planned his journey but also possible ways of losing the police if they should latch onto him. Bernard looked after Bernard, he had never had many friends but he was a type man that seemed to know everybody a little bit, and everybody knew him. When it came down to it, they really knew nothing about him. Being a car thief he had always had to rely on contacts but he did never have any of close friends, because he never trusted them, he always believed that they would give him up to save themselves, so he never gave them any details that they could give up. He decided he would find a pub and have a few beers in the way of compensation for losing the BMW sale. Also if he could get talking to somebody fairly quickly them maybe he could convince them that he'd been talking to them when the police officers were killed that way he would have some sort of alibi should he ever need one, it would be better than nothing. He found a quiet pub a few streets away and after few moments got talking to a dark head bearded bloke. This meeting would change his lifestyle completely.

He had just let Max.

Max had just found his next convert.

Chapter 12

OVER THE NEXT SIX months Max kept himself busy lining up people to join the Guild, it was surprising how easy it was to find people, the right kind of people, once you became friendly and accepted by one or two shady people you then tended to meet their friends, and their friends. Max was very fussy about the people that he selected. The people that he selected he picked because of their total lack of feelings. They were people who were capable of putting a knife into somebody just for the loose change in their pockets. At the same time, they were not the sort if people that did things without thinking, the people he had selected were full-time professional criminals, some people might call them the scum of the earth, but not to their faces. At the same time, these people had an animal cunning and a good knowledge of the particular trades that they had taken up. Among these people, there were burglars, people who were expert with alarms and electronics experts, people capable of tuning a car engine to perform 50 percent better. There were armed robbers, bank robbers, kidnappers and con merchants Max was very aware that with all these people waiting to join there would be a glut of murders. That of course would wake the police up to the idea that something was happening, and that the last thing that Max wanted now.

This problem worried Max for a long time. He eventually decided that the best way to carry out the initiation of new members would be to travel up and down the country that way only a couple of members would take the initiation in each police division. There was of course a danger of the police putting all the murders together, it did not matter how or when and some bright copper might just link them as the work of one organisation. He decided that rather than wait for one of the other Grandmasters release he would initiate some of them himself. In addition, he had had time to rethink the structure of the Guild. He now no longer believed it possible for just the three Grandmasters to run the Guild. In coded Letters to Rab and Jake, Max outlined his plans. He was going ahead with what they had worked out a long time ago and that was to recruit what you could call Sub Grandmasters, at the moment he told them he decided that two would be enough although it was possible that they might need to take on a third one. The Sub Grandmasters would still have to pay their entrance up front; part of their duties would include the filming of the new member's initiation. The Sub Grandmasters or to cut it short the Sub Masters would have to be as hard and ruthless as the Grandmasters themselves, Max thought hard and long about this and he had decided after consultations with Rab and Jake that Sally and Bernard would make good Sub Masters, provided that they pass the initiation without any hesitation. They would also be groomed to take the places of the Grandmasters should any mishap befall them.

Max and Sally had become quite good friends spending many hours together. Much against his better judgment Max had confided quite a lot in Sally, There were a couple of evenings where they ended up in bed together and although they worked hard to give each other pleasure and relief, the vital spark that makes a good relationship sexually just wasn't there. They enjoyed it and in all probability, they would carry on doing it but more as relief rather than any great passion. Max had realised that there was no love left in him. After the first couple of TV dinners together Max thought it sensible to initiate Sally, first that way if they fell out Sally would be in no position to go to police hoping for revenge.

Sally had been having trouble with one of her pimps. Twice she had beaten him nearly to death still didn't want to play by her said a rules, he had even started to get in contact with the other pimps and was trying to get them to stand together against Sally. Strong-arm protection only works if the people paying for that protection are frightened of the collector. Once that fear goes then they have beaten the protectors, leaving them out in the cold and out of business. This situation needed sorting out straightaway. Max suggested that Sally used this pimp for her initiation. Sally would invite the pimp to a room for a meal on the pretext to discuss and their present problems, with this sorted out, Max had an idea. The pimp was going to die but it needed to be set up properly. Talking to Sally, he found out that the pimp had a special girlfriend. Both Max and Sally thought that this girl might cause trouble if she knew why her pimp to have been killed deliberately. They decided that the girl would have to die as well. With good timing, this would be quite easy, if

Sally eliminated the pimp and then Bernard eliminated the girl, that way Max would have two new members in one evening. Bernard duly contacted, after listing to the plans was quite willing to go along, as he had never had anything to do either wit the pimp or girl there was no reason for anybody to look at him with regard to their death. It all went down rather well; Sally contacted the girl the next afternoon and asked her to get a room for the night explaining that she had got a new girl that she wanted to try her out with a few men. This was nothing unusual as it was a normal way that Sally took on new girls. The girl duly rented a room paid for it in advance she bought the key to Sally. Sally suggested that she might like to turn up at the room that evening at 8 o'clock and give an opinion on the girls' performance. The girl liked the thought to this, she actually thought that Sally had taken to her and that she was considering setting her up as a pimp or maybe even as a madam in a brothel. Promoted to a pimp or brothel-keeper she would have more money and as long as she kept Sally sweet, she would have a lot more power. Sally then phoned the pimp in question and arrange for him to meet her at the room at seven that evening. She told him that she had been thinking over what the future might bring and with a few minor changes; some of his points could be valid. Saying that it was possible with a few adjustments that they could come to some sort of arrangement, that would put a little bit more money in both their pockets. They could discuss them over a meal and a few beers. The pimp was more than happy with this idea he fully believed that he was finally getting somewhere with Sally. Max got into the room without being seen by anyone and set up the video camera inside a box on the sideboard. When he and Sally heard the pimp walking up the stairs Max turned the video camera on, he then placed three classes and three bottles of beer on the table, one at each end and a third one to one side halfway along the table. Bottles and glasses had been wiped clear of any fingerprints as was everything else in the room Max, set at one end of the table so that his body hid the box with the video camera in it. Sally sat in the chair half way along the table. The pimp did not even bother to knock he was so cock sure of himself that he just pushed open the door and walked in. He felt only a little surprised to see Max, Sally and Max had been a talking point among his friends for quite a while now. They took it for granted that for some reason Max was joining forces with Sally. Maybe Max had changed her mind, and had managed to talk some sense into the fucking woman. Max gestured towards the empty chair with the bottle and glass in front of it "Take the weight off your feet mate" Max said. The pimp pulled back the chair with his foot and casually sat down; he had decided to play Max and Sally at their own game. He would be cold and sullen and say very little but listen a lot. As the pimp was pouring his beer, Sally looked at Max who nodded

"I'll get some food," Sally said. With that, she got up and walked behind the pimp to the fridge,

"I don't have all night" said the pimp.

"Let us just say what has got to be said and get it over with." Sally reached into the fridge and came out with a piece of wire with a wooden handle at each end. She quickly crossed her arms to form a large loop in the wire. From behind the pimp she slipped it over his head just, as she did this Max stood up and stepped to one side, that way the video camera would recall all the details including sound. Sally and the pimp now showed in full frame of the video. Sally placed one knee in the centre of the chair back and pulled slowly and surely with all her strength on the wooden handles. The pimp was dead in less than 20 seconds and all that showed was a very thin line of blood round the man's neck. Taking a scarf that he had bought in a charity shop Max placed it around the man's neck the man now sat in a chair with his chin on his chest it looked as if he was drunk. The video in the box was the moved to the windowsill so that the lens now focused on the chair that Max had been sitting in. A quick call on the phone and Bernard came up from downstairs, Sally left the room and at eight o'clock the pimps girlfriend knocked on the door, Bernard let her in, she was surprised to find just the three men there. "What the fuck is going on?" as she said that she could see her boyfriend pimps sat in a chair with his back to her. Looking at her boyfriend, she screamed at him

"You rotten fucking bastard you're pissed again and you expect me to give freebies to these two bastards." She did not look at the pimp as she flounced into the room and sat at the end of the table and poured herself a beer,

"Wake up you fucking drunken bastard!" Max sat down in front of a video camera,

"We have a problem with your boyfriend" Max said.

"You might be able to help us." Bernard casually moved round the room until he was behind the girl. Max got up and walked over to the windowsill and casually turned on a video camera. Once the video was running, Bernard came up behind the girl and put his left arm across the front of her neck. Gripping her right shoulder at the same time, he reached his right arm round the top of her head across her forehead, and gripping it tightly pulled both arms outwards the crack of her neck breaking was really loud. Max turned off the camera and put it in his pocket, the two men quickly looked around the room to make sure that they left no traces of themselves, the door locked and the key left under the mat outside as arranged. Max now had not only two new Guild members he two new Sub Masters.

Chapter 13

Jake was the first of the remaining two Grandmasters to leave prison. As it happened there was a spare room at Max's lodgings, Jake took that room. He and Max pretended not to know each other. As far as the proprietor was concerned, they had never met before. Max and Jake now had to try to find a job for the Guild to put some money into the kitty. By chance, Jake was in a pub in the better part of the city when in walked a man he had known years ago, a man called Sidney Taft. After a few drinks in the pub, Sydney invited Jake back to his house. When they got out of the car, which was naturally a chauffeur driven Rolls-Royce Jake found himself looking back down a long driveway. Jake was very surprised to be at the front door of what looked like a terribly expensive house. Sidney could see the look on Jakes face,

"Jake that's the profits of crime, my boy." Jake grinned and shook his head of the same time.

"Looks like one of us got it wrong Sidney and somehow I don't really think it's you." Sidney put his hand on Jakes shoulder and said

"Yeah, sure, I have got a big house, lots of ground, a pretty wife, the Rolls-Royce that we've just arrived in and half a dozen other big flashy cars. Along with that I've got problems too."

"I would like your problem Sidney." Jake just could not believe how well Sidney had done. It must have been about 15 years since he had seen Sidney, then he had offered to take Jake on as a driver because he was going to begin booze cruises. Sydney had decided that that was where he thought the next great deal of money was. Jake turned him down because he thought that he

55

had something better, that something better went wrong Jake ended up doing two years in jail. Still that was water under the bridge to Jake.

"Come on then Sidney what paid for all this?"

"The last time then I saw you Jake was when I offered you a job as a driver, after you turned me down I had to get somebody else, but booze cruises were paying, and still are paying so much money they I couldn't stop. I now have 15 white vans going across the Channel each day. I supply so many shops with beer, wine, spirits and cigarettes then it is unbelievable. By now, they had walked into the house and Sidney was pouring whiskies into two very expensive cut class shot glasses. The interior the house was as expensive-looking as the outside; Sidney was not exaggerating when he boasted about the amount of money he made. After a few whiskies and general chitchat, Sidney started to explain that he was having trouble with a rival gang. Sidney had always been a villain and always would be, and now his gang had grown quite large along with his business, plus a little bit of armed robbery now and then on the side. He had come to the attention of other villains. A new breed of thugs had started up in the City. There was a gang of refugees trying to muscle in on his action. So far, the other gang had stolen two of his trucks and beaten six of his men so badly that they could no longer work for him. On top of that, a week ago he believed that they had made an attempt on his life. These people were starting to play it very rough. The attempt on his life had only failed when a young teenage yobbo stole the car that he used for his business dealings from outside one of his warehouses and tried to go joyriding. On a sharp bend at about 110 miles an hour the brakes failed and it was a young teenager that died instead of Sidney, The police found the brakes had not simply stopped working, two of the flexible brake pipes cut nearly through.

Although Sidney was quite happy to give someone a beating and he personally did not mind a bit of the rough stuff, he was not a killer, and the thought that somebody was trying to kill him was really beginning to frighten him. After all this came out Sidney put his hand on Jake arm,

"Jake let me be honest for a change, it wasn't by accident that we bumped into each other; I heard that you were out of prison, and for the last week, I have had my blokes keeping a lookout for you. When he went into that pub one of my blokes spotted you and phoned me. Would you be interested in sorting my problem out for me?" Jake looked at Sidney and was about to speak when Sidney said,

"Money is not a problem Jake; I can pay enough to let you hire some real hard bastards." Jake made it look as if he was thinking the proposition over then he said to Sidney

"I am now part of what is known as the Guild let me make a phone call it might be possible that the Guild is just what you're looking for, but I have to tell you now it will not be cheap. Naturally there is a money-back guarantee if the work undertaken is not carried out to meet the demands that you have paid for." Jake phoned Max and arranged that Max would meet Jake and Sidney in a local pub in the centre of the city in two hours' time.

When Max arrived at a pub Jake and Sidney were already there after the introduction they all sat down and made a limited amount of small talk for a while. After a few beers and then a few more beers Sidney confided to Max and Jake that he would be quite willing to pay to have the leader of this other gang done away with. This looked like being the first job for a Guild, Max and Jake held their tongues, they needed to talk this over. They took a contact number from Sidney, change the subject and carried on drinking it was just before they left that Max casually mentioned to Sidney that maybe just maybe something was possible to sort out Sidney's problem for him. They agreed to meet again at 10 o'clock the next morning in a different pub. Back in their lodgings, they spent the rest of the evening working out a plan of action.

Chapter 14

10 O'CLOCK THE NEXT morning they met up with Sidney Taft. Jake and Max had worked out almost word for word what they were going to say and what they wanted from Sidney. They needed to complete the deal and in such a manner, that nobody would ever question anything about it. Once the formalities were out of the way Jake with no preamble opened the conversation.

"It works like this; the man's actual death will be recorded on a video camera, that way you'll have real proof that the job is done. However, as not everybody is quite as honest as we are, after all, you could decide once it is done not to pay Sidney I know you well enough to know that that is not possible but others don't know you as I do. If you paid up front the person, doing the job might just take the money and run. I also know that that is not possible but you do not. Neither of you could actually go to the police to complain could you? The money will be held by the Guild Grandmasters, payment will only be made upon completion of the job to your satisfaction." Sidney could see the logic in this.

"What is it going to cost me?" Max and Jake looked at each other it had been decided that Max being a stranger to Sidney would do the talking from here on.

"The full and final total price for the job is £25,000 this money is to be held in trust by us, we represent the Guild Grandmasters. There will be no question of any police involvement. The Guild is a syndicate of men and women who are prepared to go to the outer limits to achieve the required results on anything that they undertake to do. These people, completely loyal to the Guild and have proved it. The aim of the Guild is to make crime and if you like punishment a thing of profit for them and the people who deal with them. For the Guild to survive it must be dead right and true in all its dealings with everybody. We are prepared to stand in as negotiators between different people wishing to engage professional criminals. There is a fee for our Service, it is non-negotiable and you only get the offer once. That fee is 25 per cent of the cost of the job. Now before you answer, think very carefully, if you agree to these terms and then at a later date try to back out, we will terminate you. We run under strict guidelines, that way we can supply somebody to carry out whatever activity is required, from a mild beating into a very public and painful death. Our terms are very strict, but you must agree they are very straight. Nothing will be put in writing everything depends upon word of mouth. The Guilds word is his bond and to deal with us your word must be likewise, once started there is no going back." Sidney was so shocked he just did not know what to say he had heard Max talk the night before and hadn't paid too much attention to his voice. He now realise that he was dealing with a deadly serious person who meant every word of what he said and he had no doubts in his mind that if he upset Max then he would die. The outcome of any discussions with the police would be so dire that they just did not bear thinking about. In truth this person, Max, put a fear of shit in him. Sydney had gone white and as he spoke, there was a tremor in his voice.

"Can I ask questions?" Max and Jake nodded.

"Let me just get this clear in my head. I hand over £20,000 to you plus a further £5,000 commission. You then instruct your peopled to go-ahead, they do the deed which at the same time is captured on video, you will then show me the film so that I can confirm that this is the right man, you then pay the men £20,000, the men are happy, I'm happy and you have made £5,000 for putting us together. They do not know who I am and I do not know who they are. Is that right?" Max and Jake took a good look at each other and nodded.

"Smack on the button my old son." Jakes said

"Nothing will be put in motion until we are holding the money." A new meeting was arranged for two days' time. On leaving, Sidney Jake and Max went out for lunch in a smart pub in the centre of the city they chose this one because they were not known there; it was empty which gave them the privacy that they needed. Their plan was quite simple as they were only five Guild members and one of them Rab was still in jail it meant that these two would do the killings themselves. They saw no reason to bring either of the Sub Grandmasters in at this stage also it meant that they now would have a kitty of £25,000 plus the money from Sally and Bernard and that wasn't a bad fighting fund to get them started. Overall, it had not been a bad day's work.

Chapter 15

WHEN THEY RETURNED TO the lodgings, Jake found a note had been pushed under his door it read,

"I need to see you, I have been sent by Rab. I will be in the White Horse until closing time, I know Jake by sight so I will contact you there." There was no signature or name on the note and that made Jake and Max think that the writer has been very careful even though he mentioned two names, anyone else who read the note wouldn't be able to use it against them. As there was no way that, they could contact Rab at that time of night they decided to go ahead with the meeting. Max would arrive at the pub first followed later by Jake. That way if there were some sort of trap Max would be on hand to either give Jake some sort of back-up, or deal out some instant revenge if back-up was not possible. In the pub all seemed very normal there were only three other people in the main bar when Max entered. After buying his beer he went and sat down at a corner table, the three men in the bar looked normal enough. Two men in their mid-Fifties stood at the bar talking, the third man sat at a table near the empty fireplace. The man that was sat at the table had a vaguely familiar look about him. Max was certain that this man was whom they had come to see, and he was certain that he knew him but he could not put a name to the face, or a place to the man. When Jake came in, he went straight to the bar, bought a pint of lager. He totally ignored everyone else and taking his pint, he sat with his back against a wall and from his pocket; he pulled out an evening paper and made a great show of reading the paper while he sipped his pint. Max studied the face of the man that he thought he might know the man hardly moved a muscle and Max thought he is playing this rather well. Max could see that the man was slowly looking around eyeing up the doors and other men in a room. It was then that Max notice that the man had a holdall of some sort on the floor by his legs. Max slowly and carefully moved his chair a little around the table so if the man made any sudden move for the holdall he would have it chance to take the man down before anything nasty could happen. After about 20 minutes, the man picked up his holdall and went to the bar. He ordered a fresh pint of beer and a pint of lager he carried them both to the table ware Jake sat, deliberately sitting so he was facing Jake with his back to Max, he opened the conversation with

"Now that I've seen him I remember seeing Max in the big house." Jake nodded,

"I have seen your face before, put a name to it."

"I am Tandy Marsh I was transferred to the big house about six weeks before Max got released, because I was near to the end of my sentence for armed robbery I kept my head down and associated with nobody." Jake listened and watched the man's face all the time for any signs that the maybe he was playing a part. The last thing that they wanted was interference from the law or any other gang. Max from where he was sitting could hear the conversation. Max nodded, that was Jakes signal to go ahead with the conversation. Jake looked Tandy Marsh straight in the eyes and said,

"If you kept yourself to yourself why are you so interested in meeting Max and me? Why do you know that Max and I are running mates? What makes you think that we want to know you?" Tandy Marsh was expecting these types of questions. "They have a new governor at the big house, one of those do-gooders that think we would be better off if we talk things out in front of other people. You know if we told others about the crimes that we were in for them we would realise that we had done wrong, we might reform. You and I both know that that is a load of old bollocks, all that happens is you get new ideas for new crimes. Still it was better than working. You should have heard some of the stories that we all told the fucking berk that was running the sessions. I expect he will have nightmares for fucking years. Part of the deal for being released was attending the stupid fucking meetings, after a few of these meetings I got talking to Rab. By God, that was hard work. After dozens of these bloody meetings, I told Rab that I was looking for something a bit more secure then chancing another armed robbery with a bunch of amateurs when I got out. I did not think Rab could talk so much until he started to ask so many awkward and nasty questions about my past. What I thought my future would hold, I thought I was being interviewed for "this is your life." all this talk from him was so out of character for Rab. Then I began to realise that I was being interviewed for a job. After a while Rab put the rough outlines of the Guild to me, to be quite frank at the beginning I thought that was a load of old rubbish. Then I sat down and slowly worked through it. I began to realise what you are starting is a fucking good idea. When I told Rab that I was interested, he told me the price of entry. That is some fucking price. I still have some cash stashed away so I decided to accept your terms if you will have me?" Jake finish his drink, glanced at Max and saw the other man nodding his head if Rab had really sent this Tandy because he thought he was the right man for the Guild than that was fair enough by him. Plus there was an added bonus to this situation Tandy Marsh needed to kill somebody for his initiation to the Guild and the Guild had its first job and that job required a man being killed, the two jobs could both be done at the same time, it was surprising how interesting life could be sometimes. Jake looked at Tandy and said,

"Once you start the initiation to the Guild then you cannot stop, there is no leaving the Guild unless you go out in a box or with the permission of the three Grandmasters. Are you sure you fully understand and are you prepared to live or die by our set of rules? Our Guild is going to be tighter than a fishes bottom, we want a tighter knitted group of people then any other crime syndicate that has ever been thought of or dreamt of before could ever believe possible. We intend to make it so tight that it makes the Mafia seem+ like a class of schoolchildren. There will be no turning back and as you know, there are three Parts to joining. They are the witnessed killings, the money and the small matter of a tattoo." Tandy's answer to this was to reach down and lift up the small holdall that had been by his feet; he put it on the table in front of him and pushed it across to Jake. Jake moved the holdall on to his lap so that no we could see into the bag and carefully opened the top. Inside he could see several bundles of £20 notes and a small pistol. He looked across to Max and said,

"The first step is done." Max went to the bar and bought three fresh pints he then joined Jake and Tandy. The next hour spent in small talk and gently veiled questions as the three men got to know each other. Tandy Marsh was told to meet them at the 11 o'clock the following morning in the Blue Feathers.

Chapter 16

THE ARRANGED MEETING WITH Sidney Taft went ahead as scheduled. After a few drinks and a bit of small talk Jake bought up the reason for the meeting, Jake in his usual manner did not beat about the bush.

"You got the money?" he asked.

"The money is in the bag" Sidney replied,

"But I've still got questions!" Max looked at Sidney, that look nearly made Sidney lose his nerve.

"That terms had been laid out what questions can you have?" Max voice was cold and a flat the type this sends a chill down your spine. The thing that frightens Sidney the most about Max were his eyes they were the eyes of a fanatic, or someone only just sane, cold, hard eyes they never seem to blink. Sidney found himself clutching the bag of money so tightly that his knuckles had gone white and his fingertips actually hurt where there were dug into the material.

"Max I am not backing down or anything; I really want the job done and one of your people to do it. £25,000 is a lot of money to hand over to strangers. I want to know what happens if give you the money and the jobs done, and you fail to pass it on to the people that did the job? What would happen if you just put the money in your pocket and vanished? I mean to say what can I do to ensure that did not happen?" Max and Jake looked at each other; in all honesty, the man had quite a valid point it was something that needed to be worked out fully before they entered into another contract like this one.

"The Guild is a group of people; you have come into contact with us because you want work done that you are too fucking chicken to do yourself. If you were half a man, you would have taken a shotgun and blown that prat away. Instead, you are willing to employ us to do your dirty work in exchange for your money. We make our money by doing just that. Our reputation is only as good as our actions. You are right we could run off with your money and there is not a lot you could do about it. Fair enough we would be £25,000 to the good, many of the small-time crooks probably yourself included would think £25,000 it's worth a chance after all it is a lot of money. If we did that, how long would it take word of what we had done to get round the low-life of the city? When the name of the Guild was mentioned who would want to trust us? Who would be willing to contract out another job to us? Our name would be shit we would be the laughing stock of the city and nobody would want anything to do with us. You know the type of scum that hangs around the city most of them think that they are big gangsters but they are frightened of prison frightened of getting caught in fact most of them are frightened of their own shadow. This city will be taken over by the Guild; we intend to control a hundred percent of the crime. The criminals will still make a good living once the takeover is complete. There should be no need for one criminal falling foul with another if we take your money and do your job as we have said we would then the word spreads that we are good to our word. That way we make a lot of money and people have a way of getting rid of life's little complications. Our word has to be 100 per cent right. If you cannot live with that, then take your bag of money and walk out now. No hard feelings, no comebacks if you walk out now do not come near any Guild member again. Know now that this is on pain of death. It goes without saying anything that has transpired between you and us remains sealed in your mind. Walkout now and all you have lost is time." Sidney sat there ashen-faced one leg twitching up and down making the money bag on his lap act as if it were alive. Considering that he was quite a hard person Max's words had put so much fear into him that he was close to fainting. Gathering all his courage together, Sidney said,

"Alright I can live with what you're saying it makes sense to me, and I understand if I want the job done, then I have to trust your word. One last question, what happens if the man I name offers more money to let him live and extra money to do away with me? Where does your Guild stand then?" Max and Jake had already prepared for this question and they had worked out the answer. Jake gave the answer

"We have taken a contract with you; we will carry out that contract in any way shape of form that suits us as long as you wind up with the result that you have paid for. A man could have an accident, could be could be knocked over crossing the road, he could eat something that disagreed with him and of course he can always be accidentally killed in an attempted burglary. There are dozens of ways that a man can die. We're taking a contract with you if a man tries to buy out of it then we would just take his money and keep it. He will still die if he wants to offer us a contract to kill you then we will not except it. Likewise we will not accept a contract on you from anybody that we know to be connected with him, but bear this in mind, once your man is dead and the bill paid the contract is finished if somebody else then offers us a contract on you!" Jake left it in mid air, just like that. Sidney nodded this really was frightening him but he could see no way to back out he wanted the job done. At the same time, he was terrified that somebody else might want the same sort the job done on him. This whole business with the Guild was doing something that he could not I explain. He had the feeling that the whole city was about to be put under a black cloud that would affect every criminal that he knew. He passed the bag to Max "25,000 pound in used notes in bundles of 500 just as we agreed. Also a typed list with the targets named and address, I have added some rough times of his movements that I know about." Max stared hard at Sidney

"We will trust you on the money count and I am taking it for granted you're not stupid enough to plant any bugs or tracers in this bag? You understand your movements will be followed until we have the money separated from the bag, meanwhile should anything happen to us you will be dealt with by other members." Of course that part was bluff at the moment there was only three other members and they didn't know anything about this meeting but Max decided that it might not be a bad idea for future meetings. The trouble is he would have to recruit a few more members first. Sidney refused an extra drink saying that he had to get back to his whereabouts. On parting, he said,

"Can you give me a time frame when it will be done? I would hate to be without an alibi."

"Let's just say that we suggest you cover your tracks very well for the next seven days. This is something we do not advertise as we do not require an audience." Max had no intention of telling Sydney when the job would be done there was no way that he wanted to risk walking into a trap things were going too well to make stupid mistakes.

Max and Jake met up with Tandy Marsh in the Blue Feather, Tandy was told about the job in hand and he agreed that the killing of this man would make the perfect solution to his joining the Guild.

Chapter 17

ACCORDING TO SIDNEY TAFT, the contract was to be carried out a man named Alberto Crowley. He was approximately 6 ft tall stocky build dark brown hair brown eyes. He wore a gold cross hanging from his left ear lobe and he had a prominent birthmark shaped like a small tulip on his left cheek. This description and his address along with a few notes on times and places where he might be at various times of the day had been typed on a piece of paper that accompanied the money given to them by Sidney Taft. So Max and Jake had decided that they would just use Tandy and keep the other two members out of this deal. The three of them sat in a small bar on the outskirts of the city where they could not be overheard. They needed to make their plans very carefully. They had decided that the best time to hit Alberto was when he returned to his home at the end of the day. They had driven past Alberto's house during the day to see what the lay of the land was like.

That night found them sitting in a car just down the road from Alberto's house, according to Sidney and his paperwork Alberto accompanied by his bodyguards usually arrived at the house about 10 o'clock sometimes the bodyguards went in with him although most times they left him on the doorstep once his wife had the door open. Just after 10 pm, Alberto's car pulled up and stopped outside his house, Alberto swaggered down the garden path with a bodyguard each side of him. Alberto liked to play the part of a hard violent Mr Big just in case any of his neighbours were looking out of their windows. When the door opened Max, Jake and Tandy were, surprised to see what to nice-looking woman Alberto had as his wife was framed in the

66

doorway with a light silk dressing gown on and with the light behind her they could see that she had nothing else underneath it. The bodyguards turned after saying good evening, walked back to the car and drove off. The three men waited another 20 minutes then they walked up the garden path to the front door. Max knocked hard on the glass panel of the door totally ignoring the bell and doorknocker they were hoping that Alberto would mistake them for the bodyguards and think they had forgotten to tell him something. Through a glass panel of the door, they could see Alberto coming up the hallway and it looked as if he was pulling his trousers up, they could hear him mumbling and muttering under his breath he did not seem at all happy to be disturbed. Alberto opened the front and door and found himself looking directly into the eyes of those three very hard-determined looking men.

"What do you want at this time of night?" Although he did not know any of these men, he did not intend to let them intimidate him. The leader of the three men spoke the words, "Be fucking quiet, do as you are told and don't make a fuss." Max pushed a small gun hard into Alberto's cheek forcing Alberto to walk backwards down the wall with the other two following. Tandy shut the front door and put the latch down and a chain across. The last thing they wanted was any other member of the family walking in on them. As they pushed Alberto into the lounge, they could see his wife laid out on the settee with her silk dressing-gown wide-open and her legs spread wide apart. It was obvious that they had been in the process of having sex, and by the moisture around Alberto's mouth and the way his fly was only half closed showed them what sort of sex. Tandy laughed and said, "At least the condemned man ate a hearty meal." the woman sat up quickly crossing her legs as she drew the dressing-down closed. She started to scream, Tandy quickly stepped across the room and struck her sharply across the jaw, the woman fell back in a loose tumble of arms and legs. Alberto had not said a word he knew he was in trouble. Max and Jake quickly took both of Alberto's arms and tied his elbows together behind his back. Without any thought, Max kicked Alberto across the back of the knees causing Alberto to drop to the floor in a kneeling position.

"I will pay you to get out my house, how much will it cost me to let us live?" This was what Max and Jake had been hoping for; it meant that Alberto must have quite a large sum of money here in the house. Alberto stared into Max's cold lifeless eyes, the replies that came from Max was what Alberto knew would come, in fact it was the reply that Alberto would have given if the roles had been reversed

"How much have you got?" Alberto knew it was no time to tell lies.

"In the safe I have gold and jewellery worth about £30,000 and there is £40,000 in cash, take that and let me and my wife live. I will give you another

£30,000 tomorrow to kill the man that set me up, and you know as well as I do that that man must be Sidney Taft. Max nodded and untied Alberto's arms, Alberto began to perk up as he thought he had struck a deal with Max. While Max supervised Alberta opening the safe, he only let him work the combination he did not let him open the door, which was a very wise move because there was a small automatic pistol laying just inside the safe door. Alberto's elbows were then retired behind him.

Meanwhile Jake and Tandy had lifted the unconscious woman from the settee, and out of what was sheer nastiness had stripped off her dressing gown. Laid her face down across a small table, they then proceeded to tie her hands and ankles to the table legs; this left her with her backside sticking out over the edge of the table. This would allow easy access to her pussy. Tandy had been imprisoned for a long time and given the chance he was going to make full use of this situation to relieve him self. Alberto was pushed to his hands and knees by the table. Both Max and Jake set up video cameras, Max cropped his camera so it was just covered Alberto's face and shoulders, Jakes set his camera to cover the whole scene when they were both ready they nodded to Tandy. With reluctance Tandy removed his hand from between the woman's thighs and placing a rubber glove on his right hand he took the small automatic pistol that had been in the safe and put the barrel between Alberto's eyes looking straight at Jakes camera he asked them if they were ready. As both men nodded Tandy, smiled sweetly for the camera and pressed the trigger. The gun made a small popping noise and a small round hole appeared between Alberto's eyes almost at the same time the back of his head exploded in a mass of bone, brains, gristle and blood that splashed all over the wall that was 3 ft behind him. Max and Jake stopped filming and put the video cameras away. The woman started to come round she could not see her husband for whit her head over the small table all she could see was a wall and floor. Tandy and Jake looked at Max. Jake said,

"It has been a long time since Tandy and I had a woman, it does seem such a pity to waste this one doesn't it?" Max nodded they were right it had been a long time, and as the woman had seen their faces she was going to have to die anyway.

"Leave no DNA and make it quick we don't have a lot of time!" Tandy produced a packet of condoms from his pocket "These should do the trick." Tandy dropped his trousers and it was plain for all to see that he was ready for some action, he rolled a condom on to his erect tool and using both his thumbs he pushed the cheeks of the woman's arse apart exposing her wide open pussy, as he slid his prick in she started to scream. Jake did not hesitate, down came his trousers on when the condom and he pushed his prick straight into her mouth. The woman being tied across a table with one man pushing into her pussy and another pushing into her mouth had no means of refusing; she just had to go along with it. After about five minutes, Jake looked at Tandy and said,

"Am I sweating as much as you?" Tandy grinned,

"I reckon that it's time we changed ends don't you Jake? " Jake laughed,

"That's a damned good idea. We can show this slag what a proper spit roasts feels like. "The two men changed backwards and forwards until they both had had enough. While this was going on Max had removed the money and jewellery from the safe, he then went through the rest of the house tipping out draws and generally ransacking the place to make it look as if Alberto had caught them in the act of a burglary. When he came back, downstairs the two men had removed their condoms and were wrapping them in tissue paper from a kitchen roll. Tandy looked up at Max and said,

"No DNA Max."

The woman still tied to the table and now weeping softly,

"You both had enough?" Jake and Tandy both nodded. Max walked to stand beside the head of the woman. Without saying a word, he took a handful of her hair and lifted her head up and backwards, the woman made no noise apart from a slight gurgle, as the knife in Max's hands slid across her throat. The blood from the woman formed a large puddle on the floor beside her dead husband. As they left the house, they turned the lights off and dropped the latch on the door. Inside the car, Max phoned Sidney Taft

"Sidney, you need an alibi for tonight, it's all going to happen in half an hour." He did not wait for Sidney to say anything he switched off the phone. Max drove the car round the block and they parked again at the end of the road about 80 yards away from Alberto's house. This was the only way that they could think of to check Sidney's integrity. They sat there in complete silence for three-quarters of an hour. If the police had turned up it would have been a death warrant for Sidney. When no police turned up Max took the tape from his camera and put it into a stamped addressed envelope that he had already prepared. As they drove past a post box, he popped it in then drove down to the local harbour. There they opened a small bag that contained the contents of Alberto's safe. Taking out the money they put in the small automatic, after it had been wiped for fingerprints. They all looked at the pretty jewellery. It was a great temptation to keep some of it, unfortunately although that sort of thing was worth cash. All three of them knew that this type of thing was traceable. People always seem to recognise and have proof of purchase of that type of thing. It all went back into the bag, which was then thrown as far as possible into the sea from the harbour wall. Max looked at the other two and said,

"Before we leave here make sure you have bought nothing from the house." Jake shook his head while Tandy said all I bought was the memory of a damned good Fuck!"

The newspapers had a field day, Alberto known as a local crook and even the papers did not believe this to have been a simple robbery that could have gone wrong, leading to the rape and murder. The main front-page stories were,

"Gang war starts with killing of gang boss." There was a large article running the police down for letting crime get so out of hand. Even although Alberta was a crook, that he shot, his wife raped and killed, was a disgrace. The police could do nothing about it. They had no idea who they were looking for or why the crime was committed. What could be the outcome of Alberto's death? There was the normal response by the do-gooders saying that Alberto and his wife had profited and lived by the proceeds of crime all their lives so therefore it was no great thing that they had suffered its ultimate penalty at the hands of other criminals, and that nobody should spare much thought for them. There was another article suggesting that this was not a gang war but the beginnings of a war embarked on by a group of vigilantes that intended to clear up the crime in the City. Yet another version put forward was the theory that a group of Englishmen had decided to rid the county of immigrants.

Sidney Taft was over the moon he really did not need any video of the death because the police had already questioned him about it, so it proved that the right man had died. Still it gave him great satisfaction to know that he had had his moneys worth. When he saw the video of Alberto's brains being blown from the back of his head as far as he was concerned they Guild had lived up to their part of the bargain, and he would be happy to recommend them, but only to his trusted near friends.

Chapter 18

THE DAY THAT RAB was released from prison he was met by Jake and Max the three friends went first to a posh hotel where they had booked Rab a room. After that, a nice long relaxing bath and the luxury of being, shaved by a barber, then they sat around the table in the room with a bottle of whisky and three shot glasses. Rat told them that he needed to go up to Glasgow for a few days as he had some business that he needed to get out of the way. Max and Jake immediately offered to accompany him in case he needed back up.

"It's not that kind of business." Rab said,

"My mother died a few months ago and one of her old friends paid for the funeral. In addition, I have a little bit stashed away that I need to retrieve. I can get that and pay off my debt that same time." He intended to fly the next day. Jake grinned as he pulled out his mobile phone and sent a text message,

"Well that's all right, you still have plenty of time." There was a quick rap on the door Jake jumped up and opened the door very quickly, and in walked to very attractive young women. Max stood up looked at Rab and said,

"We will make sure you get an early call in time to catch the plane, meanwhile have fun with the compliments of the Guild and Sally." Rab for once was speechless, he kept looking at the girls and then understanding appeared in his eyes a large lecherous grin made his eyes sparkle now he understood why Max and Jake and said it was not necessary to get dressed. Another knock at the door and in walked a waiter with a heated dinner trolley. Rab was now set for the night not only had he got a beautiful meal that helped take away the taste of prison but he also was in the company of two young nubile women who would make up for the lonely nights that he had spent in prison. Rab realise that although he was about to start a very new life he was starting it with two of the best friends he would ever have.

The next day feeling totally, relaxed Rab stepped onto a plane heading for Glasgow. He arrived at his mother's house and went straight to the master bedroom prised up the carpet in one corner of the room, and lifted a short loose floorboard. This revealed a slam shut safe it was with relief that he realised that the safe had not been touched. He had bought the house for his mother many years before, at the time Rab had been an honest man but for some reason he did not want put the house deeds in his own name. He put the deeds in the name of a fictitious company, later he registered that company and made himself the sole proprietor. When he was arrested and the police are searching for money that he had stolen they totally missed the fact that he owned this house. His mother had always told people that she lived in the house rent-free as part of her pension for working for the same company for 45 years. Rab opened the safe and removed tight bundles of money altogether there were £60,000. His face distorted into a look of sadness, when he had stashed the money there £60,000 had been a lot of money for the future. Unfortunately, 60,000 pound was not enough to make up for the years of imprisonment that he had suffered. He was holding in his hands all that remained of the millions of pounds that he had stolen; this was the only money that the police had not recovered. Still there was more than what most people had and he was about to have money coming in from the Guild.

Rab went next door but one to see Amy, this was his mum's friend that had paid for the funeral and made sure that his mother had a good send-off. While he was drinking a cup tea with Amy, she told him about his mother's last few months. Amy thought his mother had just given up the will to live. It came as news to Rab that in the last few months of her life his mother's house burgled twice. Apparently, a gang of young lads on the estate that had taken great delight in making life miserable for his mother and a few other old age pensioners. Amy included. Rab kept his temper and as he talked to Amy, he gave her the impression there was nothing he could do about it. He gradually found out from her where this group of blokes liked to hang out. Rab paid Amy the money that he owed her for the funeral plus enough money to allow Amy to have a good holiday at her sister's house just outside Fort William. Just to make sure that she was going Rab phoned for a taxi, and when it came, he paid the driver to take Amy immediately to her sister's house. As she, left Amy was crying with gratitude and saying what a wonderful son Rab had been to his mother.

Rab walked round the estate until he came to a place where Amy said the gang hung out. Rab then went into town and booked a flight back to the city for that evening. He went into two charity shops before he found a cheap raincoat and hat that fitted him. He hired a car, drove back to the estate and waited until dusk settled in. As he waited, he watched a group of young men gather under the overpass bridge. Dressed in the Mac and hat from the charity shop Rab walked towards the young men looking essentially as if he was drunk, at the same time he was counting quite a large bundle of money. The young lads could not believe their luck the six of them stepped out from under the bridge and formed a line in front of Rab. Rab kept up the pretence of being drunk,

"Hello lads, how's it going?" the men looked at each other.

Not only was this bloke a drunk and load with money but he was stupid as well. The leader of the group stepped forward just as Rab put the money back in his pocket,

"Don't put that money away mate, it will save you a lot of pain and trouble if you just handed it over to us now." Rab looked at the bloke and in a quiet sober voice said,

"You and your fucking mates were responsible for killing my mother, now it's time for you to die." The young man's face went slack and his mouth fell open. Before he could say anything Rab struck. The first two fingers of Rabs right hand took out the young lads eyes. As the man doubled over screening Rab stepped forward and with a sharp chop of the edge of his left hand, he struck one of the other men across this side of the neck the man dropped as if he had been pole axed. Rabs right foot struck out in a sideways motion taking the third man across the front of his right shin, as the man doubled over Rabs knee took him in the face and the man's head shot upwards and backwards and smashed into the face of the man behind him. By this time, one of the remaining men had pulled a knife. Rab spat straight in his face. The man automatically closed his eyes and that was when Max kicked straight between the legs. As the man started to curl over he grabbed the knife from his hand and with a stabbing motion pushed the knife into the soft lower stomach of the last man standing, then he twisted the blade and drew the blade as far as he could towards a man's chin. Quite calmly, Rab cut the throats of each of the remaining five. All this had taken less than three minutes, from start to finish. Rab cut a square from one of the men's T-shirts and used it to wipe the knife clear of prints. He then used the bloodstain piece of cloth to wrap around the handle of the knife. Rab then sank the blade into the leader's stomach, using his lighter he set fire to the rag and watched it burn. He then discarded the blood stained Mac and hat into a nearby skip and went back to the car. Rab was in plenty of time for his flight away from Glasgow.

Chapter 19

THE MEETING OF THE six members of the Guild held in the backroom of a small dingy pub in the centre of the city. Max as founder member of the Guild chaired the meeting.

"When I first thought of the Guild I envisioned a group of people that committed different crimes for other criminals for a price. I could also see us starting gang wars and hiring our services to both sides, making a lot of money by assassinating different gang members. Over the last, few weeks I have come to realise that this might be a little bit of an idyllic way of thinking. I do still believe that we should hire ourselves out as assassins provided the price is right. I now believe that after looking at the criminals in this city that we as a Guild should start thinking about taking over the whole criminal element of this city." The others were very shocked by Max's statement.

"You mean the six of us should run the whole bloody city? I thought that we were going to just control part of it." Rab really liked the idea,

"Instead of hiring out to those low-life bastards, why don't we just takeover what they're doing? We could run their businesses with them doing the work and us collecting the money. In a city there is quite a thriving sex market also there is a good opportunity for a protection racket among the large amount of restaurants and clubs. It would not take a lot to takeover most of the drug business if not all of the."

"I have done a lot of hard thinking since we started this" Max was not sure how to put the rest although he had killed several people in the last few years he was not a long-term criminal. He had been a law-abiding man up until the death of his grandchildren.

"I believe the idea of taking over the crime in this city is the way forward for us. The only thing that I'm not very keen on is the drugs trade. I have no objections to killing or maiming the normal sort of low life that is walking the streets of this city. If people like us deal with that sort of scum then the normal good citizen does not cause us too much trouble. If we are going to drugs then, to Mr average citizen, seeing children that are addicts then puts us on the same level as the scum that is doing it now. Next Mr Average starts trying to get rid of us."

"Drugs will be sold on the streets of this city. That is a fact it does not matter if it is us or somebody else they will still be sold. There is a lot of money to make. If we controlled the drug trade, and I say that we should do it, and do it properly then your Mr Average citizen will have no knowledge that we are involved in it. We takeover those that run the drugs trade and in turn run them." What Rab said make sense even Max had to concede that.

"OK if we are going to run the drugs then let's do it right, by making them as safe as we can without losing any of the prophet. By controlling the way that the drugs are cut, if you like we could say that we were cleaning up the drugs trade." Sally who was always ready to increase her wealth asked

"Six of us, is that enough to control a whole city? Somehow, I do not think so! With a few more members, or should I say the right sort of members maybe we could."

"Max you drop this in our laps without warning, but knowing you, you have already worked out how to do it. Am I right?" Tandy had come to know Max well enough to realise that Max was a man that sorted things out before he opened his mouth. Max replied made all the others reach for their classes.

"I propose that we conduct the takeover this city with complete and utter violence. At the moment as we only have one small pistol between the six of us that we arm ourselves, for now by raiding one of the local police stations. This is going to kick-start our reputation as a hard team not to be tangled with. If we tried to buy weapons, either people would try to sell us rubbish or knowing our identity, they will shop us to the local police. If we take on a police station the way I plan to do it we will only gain a few weapons, but the very fact that we have taken them from the police station will enhance our reputation giving us a lot of credibility among the other criminals. The thing is to get away with it entirely we must be prepared to kill anyone that can identify us. That will bring the full wrath of the police down upon us, knowing this I suggest that we return here tomorrow evening at the same time. After we have had the day thinking about it, vote as to whether we will go ahead with it. So far, I have planned the job and I believe it will be quite simple. To go forward with this plan I am thinking it is only fair that being a job of this magnitude we should have a unanimous vote. If one person is against it then we forget it and move on to something else." The whole group were silent, nobody moved, they all realise that if they went ahead with this idea then there could be no possibility of turning back and once the ball started rolling there could be no stopping it. They could stay as minor villains or they could take the whole city. In fact, it was all or nothing.

The next evening found the six of them in the same pub sitting round the same round table, again Max opened the proceedings.

"Before anybody says anything let me outline the procedures rather than have a debate that would go backwards and forwards all night, I have here too small pot's one of which I will put in the middle of the able and the other will stand on the mantelpiece that way nobody can see into it. I also have 12 pieces of paper that are all the same size, 6 are blank and six have a black cross on them. Each of you will have one each of these papers we will then stand in a line. One at a time we will walk past the table and put one piece of paper in that pot then the second piece of paper will then go into the pot on the mantelpiece. If all six papers that have the black cross on them are in the pot on the table then we go ahead with a raid on the police station, if one is missing then the deal is off. If somebody were not in favour of the idea then it would be wrong for any of the rest of us to criticise him or her. Now we six, Rab Jake and I will make most of the decisions with the help of you three. Once we have got round to recruit new members that are waiting to be initiated then all the decisions would be by Jake Rab and myself with the possibility of a little bit of input from you Sally Bernhard and Tandy. We will form the main hub of the Guild. The rest of the members will be the normal soldiers."

Max took the pot from the table and turned it upside down unfolded the six pieces of paper and laid them out in a line. On the table, six pieces of squared paper each showing a black X. The twelve bits of paper burnt in an ashtray. "Now I do believe it is time to get down to business. This operation must go like clockwork." So far, Max had managed to form a group of people that had melded themselves into one family unit all with the same convictions and ideals. In fact, Max had made what can only be called the perfect killing machine. The basic plan was to create three diversions, which would necessitate the involvement of the maximum amount of police officers. This would leave the police station with no one in attendance until reinforcements from stations in other districts arrived. In that time the police station could be entered and whatever weapons were left in the arms store would be removed. So far they had kept a very low profile and although the law new something was happening they did not know who to look for. Life for the Guild was about to change, the police would no longer be able to push a crime aside thinking it was only criminals against criminals and that no member of the public was being harmed. The police would now be aware that a new kind of criminal was in the City, The police station was chosen it was like most police stations desperately undermanned and terribly overworked it barely had enough men to cover the three districts that it controlled on a good day. On a bad day, it was the practice to call officers in for support from the other local police stations. The first thing that the Guild did was cause a small disturbance in one of the market precincts. At the right time three men ran out of a notorious pub shouting

"He's got a fucking gun." Naturally a member of the public phoned the police reporting that a gunman was killing people in the precinct. The police duly turned up covered in bulletproof equipment. Max listening in on a scanner timed their arrival and the arrival of the reinforcements at the police station it took the police 15 minutes to get to the market and 25 minutes for the reinforcements to get to the station.

Three days later, using a few of Sallie's people, three incidents spread the police very thin on the ground. These diversions had been set up to keep the police busy.

Reported to the police was a large container that the caller feared might be a bomb. It was found near a school with 500 children in attendance who were about to come out for lunch. This container could be heard ticking also there was a dark brown substance leaking from one corner.

A few minutes after the phone call, the police were informed that three men carrying pistols were seen getting out of a car next to a shopping precinct.

To make matters worse a woman phoned and told the police that six armed men had just kidnapped a small child and its mother in a car and had driven into the local park, the park was full of people. These phone calls had surprising enough come from each of the three different districts controlled by the police station. The police station was now down to four men, a sergeant on the main desk a civilian who was in charge of the arms store and property Office, and two men left in the cad room. Within two minutes, of the last police officer leaving the station a young girl walked into the reception area, she was sobbing and her dress was torn. As the desk sergeant pulled back, the glass panel to talk to the girl, three men walked through the door. Totally ignoring the girl, they stood reading the posters on the wall with their backs to the desk sergeant. As soon as the sergeant opened his mouth to talk to the girl she promptly collapsed on the floor. The sergeant could do no more than unlock the door and come out to help her, as he bent to pick the girl up, one of the men smashed him across the back of the head with a short piece of pipe filled lead. The sergeant collapsed to the floor in a pool of blood. If he survived the blow then he would not be much help as a witness because he had not seen any of the men's faces. Rab was left in the front office to let the girl leave, and then he locked the front door. After doing this, he dragged the sergeant through to his office and laid him under the desk he then put the sergeant's jacket on and unlocked the door. He then sat at the desk anyone who had came in the door would be informed that the police station was closed for the rest of the day, unfortunately this was not an unusual event. While Rab waited for the other two, he busied himself by removing the video from the CCTV camera covering the front desk. Max and Jake found that the station was empty apart from the two people in the cad room; these people were so busy with incoming calls and radio transmissions that they did not notice Max and Jake. They found the small armoury door was still open, and the counter was down where the man had been issuing weapons. A civilian was in the process of tidying up the paperwork as he heard footsteps of the two men approaching he pulled open the weapons issue book and looked up thinking that a couple of CID offers had come to draw weapons. There was no hesitation Max swung his arm, the homemade cosh crashing down across the bridge of the man's nose. The man collapsed onto the floor bleeding heavily through his nose. Max and Jake looked at each other and without a word Jake pulled a stiletto from his boot and cut the man's throat. On looking round the armoury they realise just how few weapons the police station actually had. They had known that a lot of them would have been it out because of the false alarms that they had set up. All that were left were three rifles which weren't a lot of good to them because they were so hard to conceal and four pistols, it was better than nothing the pistols would have to do. They managed to find two boxes of ammo to go with the Pistols. They strode back through the station past the cad room to the front entrance from the time the sergeant had bent to pick up the girl until they reach the front door on their way out only seven minutes had passed.

Once again, the newspapers had a field day. A dead police officer and a dead civilian employed by the police plus four pistols and ammunition missing from a police station that was left so undermanned that people would walk in and help themselves. The police did not even know how many people were involved in the robbery and they had no clues as to who they were. The police were really running around like a dog chasing its tail. Large sums of money offered to the grasses and informants of course brought in nothing, nobody knew anything. The only person outside the Guild that could give evidence and prove what had happened was the young girl that had collapsed in the office and it was very unfortunate that she died within minutes of leaving the police station, compliments of Tandy.

Chapter 20

IT WAS DECIDED THAT the weapons they had accumulated so far were OK but should one of the members be caught with them, because of the way they were acquired it would bring the Guild a lot of grief. The raid on the police station at first glance seemed to be extremely foolish; it had put the police in an awkward situation. The only way the police could prove their integrity was to bring some belated justice for the raid on the police station. On the other hand, the underworld was buzzing about the type of person that must have committed that raid. The talk in the underworld had turned these people into near enough Super heroes. Word of the Guilds actions were spreading, but so far, not even the cleverest grass in the City could find out anything that could remotely implicate the Guild in the raid on the police station. The rumours among the low life of the city were rife and so the Guild seemed to be drawing all the credit for the raid without any of the investigation. The credibility of the Guild had increase so much that some of the bigger fish in the criminal fraternity ranks were seeking out the Guild to join, or to use their services. Now that they had the attention of the right people, they needed to press their point.

The plan all along had been to carry out work for other criminals at a price, specialist teams could be put together from the Guild members to perform jobs that normal criminals weren't capable of doing or hadn't got the bottle to do. Now the Guild had changed its aims and intended to takeover crime in the entire city. Jake of all people came up with the ideal way to supply weapons for the Guild. Jake had always admitted that he was more muscle than brain but what he was about to say was such a good idea that the rest of them let him talk.

"There is an army camp just outside the city it is a main REME workshop. 20 miles away from that there is an ammunition dump; we could do both of these at the same time. Now the army's security is rather lax if we do just one of these camps than the security will become so tight that nobody would be able to steal mouse shit from the other one we only get one chance and I think that we should hit both camps at the same time. The army guards are easy now and although they carry rifles, I happen to know that because we are in England they do not have the ammunition loaded in the magazine that is on the rifle. The three Grandmasters then set about planning the double raid, they worked out what they wanted and it was like a shopping list.

The main weapon would be the Browning 9 mm semi-automatic pistol. Because the magazine holds 13 rounds, with one up the spout that gives the user 14 rounds. Not wide and it is reasonably small so that it can be concealed without producing too much of a lump about the person. The Browning 9 mm is a tried and tested weapon of many years' standing with very few faults. It was normal to discard a weapon once used for a killing; this necessitated getting used to a new weapon plus of course the fact of spending money and risking discovery getting another one. Spare parts could be stolen with the pistols, and where better to get spare parts than a REME workshop. Replacing the barrel and firing pin after use would mean that the owner could keep using the pistol, which was familiar to him. Off-course a barrel and firing pin can be disposed of much easier than a complete pistol. A single barrel and firing pin would be easy to hide away. Used in connection with an additional crime, by a different person, leading the police to believe that one man had committed a string of crimes. If a Guild member decided to give evidence against the Guild, then the Barrel and firing pin from a serious crime, planted on them for the police to find, that way they would lose all credibility. The police would think it better to wipe out all crimes committed with that barrel and firing pin, than follow up the evidence of the grass. Each member was aware of this at his or her initiation.

The second weapon of choice was the Sterling SMG, a short robust weapon with a butt that can be folded back along the barrel, again an easy weapon to conceal under an overcoat or Macintosh. The SMG had two firing modes, single-shot and automatic. On cocking the weapon the breach block with a fixed firing pin was held back by the trigger, when the trigger was pressed the block would push forward picking up the first round from the magazine. The round pushed into the breach, as the breach closed the firing pin struck the rear of the round and fired weapon. The recall pushed breechblock back the empty case was ejected and the breechblock engaged on the trigger if set a single shot. If set for automatic the breechblock came forward by itself the SMG carried on firing until either the trigger was released or the magazine was empty. Again, the ammunition was 9 mm and by choosing these two weapons, only one type of ammunition was necessary. However, with all the members using the same weapons there was no need for dozens of different types of ammunition, if one member ran short of ammo for any reason he could use ammunition from somebody else. Also using one type of ammunition for both weapons required a lot less consideration for storage. Once again changing both the barrels and breach blocks turned the weapon into a new one. Once again the SMG had been in service with the British army for a long time and had proved itself time after time.

It would take all current members of the Guild to carry out the raids on the army camps. By normal standards both these types of weapons were considered to be fairly old and nearly past their best, that these weapons had proved their worth were important to the Guild also, they were a lot less complicated to maintain than the more modern weapons.

Chapter 21

MAX STOOD IN THE shadows not far from the entrance to the REME workshop from where he was he not only had a clear view of the guardroom but he could hear the conversation between the drivers and the sentries on gate duty. At 3 am, a Land Rover stopped by the guardroom the sentry came out to check the driver and his mate.

"Where the fucking hell are you going at this time of night?"

"That fucking prat of an officer, in his wisdom has decided that he wants us to go and get him a fucking pizza." The driver did not sound very happy,

"I have only had 10 minutes sleep all fucking night. That stupid little bastard officer keeps sending me out, he seems to think that he is making my stint as duty driver interesting and rewarding. Still you're alright in the warm; these Land Rovers are so draughty it would be no colder if they didn't have the top on."

"Hey you're right the guardroom is warm but it is as a bloody nuisance coming-out to check on you drivers."

"I will only be 10 minutes the smart bastard ordered it on the phone and I'm only picking it up. When I come back I'll flash my highlights once and sound my horn twice then you will know it's me."

"That's a great idea and that will save me coming out in the cold again."

Max was straight on his mobile to Jake,

"A Land Rover with two men, when they come back in 10 minutes they will flash their lights once and honk their horn twice." Max put the phone away he did not even wait for a reply.

Just as the Land Rover rounded the first corner, the driver could see a man, who was collapsed in the road,

"Another drunken squaddie that didn't quite make it to the camp I reckon." The driver's mate said.

"We had better stop and give him a lift back to camp it will save the poor sod getting charged in the morning for being drunk and disorderly." The driver pulled the Land Rover to a stop by the collapsed man, as he started to climb out of the cab; he was struck across the head viciously from behind. The driver's mate hearing the man fall leant across the driver's seat to see what had happened, he found himself looking straight into the eyes of Jake, the lead waited pipe took him on the side of the jaw causing him to collapse immediately. The two men quickly stripped of their combat jacket and head gear. Bernard looked at Jake and said,

"He saw your face!" Jake reached for the stiletto in his boot and without hesitation slit the soldier's throat.

"What about his mate?"

"He did not see anything" Jake replied. With the two soldiers dumped into the ditch at the side of the road Jake and Bernard quickly put on the combat jackets, head gear, and jumped into the front of the Land Rover. By this time, Max had reached the scene and after a quick look around and with a nod to the two men, he jumped into the back of the Land Rover. As they approached the guardroom they could see the sentry looking out of the window, Bernard flashed their lights, honked his horn twice and drove straight into the camp. They soon found the armourers shop, this was the place where the other army camps sent their small arms for repair when their own regimental armourers did not have the facilities to repair them themselves. The army being the army had no burglar alarms; instead, the army relied on to sentries walking the beat for two hours at a time. In the cold wet wind and rain, as it was this night. Bearing in mind that the sentries were, only human, did what patrolling sentries have always done. They had hidden themselves in the back of a truck, to have a quiet cigarette. After all, who in their right mind robs an army camp? At worse, you might get some drunken squaddie wandering about where he should not be. That was about all sentry duty in the eyes of most British soldiers in peacetime is, it's a dull and boring experience an extra guard duty is quite often given as a punishment for minor infringements of the army regulations. The door to the armoury shop was soon forced. Max was the first one in and the first thing he did was turn all the lights full-on, with the Land Rover outside and the shop door wide open with the lights on inside too men in combat jackets being handed weapons by a civilian would cause no comment even if the guard did see them. It really did look as if a unit was making a late collection of repaired weapons from the armourers shop.

Everything had been set to make things look natural. A quick search found the rack of weapons that they wanted. About 60 Browning 9 mm pistols were chained together on one rack in of the storeroom, these weapons had been newly rust proofed and repaired and were waiting for collection. A bolt cutter took care of the padlocks on each end of the chain released the Pistols. Bernard and Jake quickly put pistols into boxes and carried them out to the Land Rover. Meanwhile Max went into the rust proofing room and boxed up a couple of hundred Browning magazines these were taking out to the Land Rover with the pistols Jake and Bernhard returned went into the storeroom, and boxed up every Browning barrel and firing pin that they could find. Then they boxed up three boxes of spare parts not that they knew what the parts belong to but it would help to make it look like a professional raid. All three returned to the weapons rack where they found about 40 Sterling sub-machine guns known as SMG these were quickly added to the stock in the Land Rover along with magazines barrels and breach blocks, Max had turned out the lights and closed the door and then he got into the back to the Land Rover. As they drove towards the guardroom, Bernard flashed his lights and honked his horn twice. The guard gave him a big grin and the thumbs-up sign from the window and off they went. From driving into the camp to driving back out of they camp almost 20 minutes had passed. The two sentries were still in the back of the truck having a smoke, thinking all was well in their world. It was for the time being. The Guild now had a collection of weapons that would see them through anything they wanted to handle.

Chapter 22

AT THE SAME TIME that the other three had hit the workshop, Rab Tandy and Sally were outside the ammunition dump. They had been there waiting for a call from Max to say that things were starting to kick-off at his end.

They had identified the bunker that held the 9 mm rounds a few days before. They had been lucky enough to come across a couple or soldiers that worked in the ammo dump in one of the local pubs. They were so drunk that the conversation they had had with a young girl who kept asking them about ammunition.

Once they had the call from Max it would be a simple operation of getting in and taking the ammunition that they required and getting out. Two sentries were patrolling the grounds of the compound, which has made up of a series of grass and earth covered bunkers set out with 50 yards between each one, this in the hope that any fire would not be able to jump the gap. In fact, this was the key to the whole operation; the compound was surrounded by a large barbed-wire fence. Each bunker was floodlit by some very heavy lighting.

Because the area where the ammunition dump was secluded it was quite common for courting couples to come out to park for a chat and of course a quick screw. The sentries considered it as one of their rewards to spy on courting couples and if there was anything interesting to watch, they had an arrangement of signals so that all the other guards could come and have a look as well. Sally had arranged for one of her pimps to set up a little tabloid that would keep the guards well and truly happy and occupied. The pimp was told that it was one of these guards' birthdays and because he was on duty, his mates had clubbed together and paid for a treat for him. The pimp was told to take two of his girls to the ammunition dump and park near the fence, which happened to be on the other side of the compound from the bunker that the Guild were interested in. The girls would then get out of the car and in their very skimpy clothes would start to have an argument that was to turn into a catfight showing plenty of their thighs and naked boobs. The fight would gradually turn into a lesbian torrid affair. The beginning of the argument would be the signal for the young guard to come and see what was happening to the girls. Once the pimp was certain that all guards were attracted to the fight he had to get both girls to make friends. He would then get them to strip off and put on a sex show with him and each both girls. This of course would keep the two sentries to one side of the compound away from the bunker with the ammunition in it. Everything went well, the two guards sat on the side of another bunker watching one man and two women that were all naked having sex on the ground in front of a car.

Rab Tandy and Sally cut through the wire on the opposite side of the compound and crossed to the door of the bunker that they wanted; Tandy quickly used the bolt croppers to cut through the hasp of the padlock on the door with only a minimum of sound. Any sound was masked by the squeals, laughter and gasps coming from the group in front of a car.

All three of them had torches and foldaway shopping trolleys that booze runners use when they bring back beer from France. As soon as they were in the bunker they quickly found the 9 mm boxes and loaded up their trolleys, they quietly made their way back to the hole in the wire with the boxes, which were neatly stacked in a small pile. They then went back in and loaded up again and this time as they left they closed the bunker door and fitted a brand-new padlock to it. Then they went back to the pile of boxes and quietly loaded all of them into the boot of a large car. The piece of wire that had been cut away to make the hole in the fence was put back and held in place with some galvanised wire, that way when the guards returned to their beats they would not notice that the compound had been breached. They coasted the car down a small slope until they were clear of the compound it was then that they started the car and drove into the night. In 15 minutes, they had managed just to steal 20,000 rounds of 9 mm ammunition.

Chapter 23

THE DRIVER OF THE army Land Rover laid out in the ditch next to the dead passenger. For the first few minutes, he was only just conscious and his brain would not let him work out what had happened. Then it came to him, a drunken squaddie laid out in a road and he remembered starting to get out with the intention of helping him. After that he could remember nothing, sitting up he started to shake his mate,

"Come on wake up for Christ's sake, wake up. What the hell are we doing here?" It was then that he realise his mate was not breathing. It wasn't until he was bending over spewing his last meal, that his head began to hurt, very carefully with shaking fingers he felt the side of his head and he found a great soggy mass where he had been clubbed. He managed to staggered to a phone box about 200 yards down the road from there he phoned the guardroom. It had never entered his head to phone the police, he took it for granted that although he thought the duty officer was a prize prat at least he would know what to do about his dead mate. The duty officer took charge and in a second Land Rover and with two of the nights guards quickly found the driver and his dead mate.

When the police were eventually called which must have been a good half-an-hour after the driver first became fully conscious they were not very happy. As far as the police could see, they had nothing really to go on, the driver had seen nobody, only the blurred shape of a man lying face down in the road, the passenger might have seen some thing but he was dead, and he was dead for reasons best known to the killers themselves. This really was going to be a tough one to crack. The Land Rover was found just before dawn, it had been burnt out and there was no chance of any fingerprints or other type of evidence, and of yet any sign of a motive for the crime.

Just before Reveille the soldier that had been in charge of the gate plucked up his courage. He told the duty officer that he had allowed a Land Rover in and out of the camp without going s outside to check the driver or passenger, because he had arranged with the driver to give a signal when he approached the barrier. The duty officer called out the guard immediately instructed them to search the workshop compound for any signs of a break-in it was then that they found the forced door on the armourers shop. That was when the motive for the crime became quite clear. The army needed a scapegoat, and the police needed a scapegoat, someone must be blamed. The Amy selected the guard and blamed him for not checking the Land Rover properly, while the rest was blamed on the passenger of the Land Rover, the army and police decided that he must have been the inside man, and that for some reason upset the gang. The police put the blame on their failure to apprehend criminals squarely at the feet of the Land Rover driver. If he had phoned the police as soon as he regained consciousness then the police would surely have caught the criminals in the act. What the police didn't realise was the fact that by the time the driver regained consciousness the weapons were well hidden and the Land Rover had not only been dumped but had already been burnt out.

The natural hostilities between the police the army caused many bad feelings and co-operation between the two units was near enough non-existence. The army objected to the police running all over the compound, the police objected to the army trying to use the military police to chase civilian criminals; at least the police thought they were civilians. The news that the ammunition dump raided as well did not come in until after breakfast, because of the raid on the workshop, the other compounds had to be inspected as a matter of course, and it was eventually found that the padlock on one of the bunkers had been changed and nobody had a key for it.

The papers had a field day they speculated that it was a terrorist gang that had armed itself for dirty deeds throughout the country and if not Europe. From every angle, that they looked at nobody could understand why the driver lived and the passenger died. This one part baffled both the police and the papers. What nobody would tell them was that although the Guild was capable of extreme violence and would kill any one, man woman or child that could identify them; they had no desire to kill for the sake of killing. Any other gang committing this crime would probably have been content just to render the two men unconscious and if the passenger tried to identify anyone then he or his family would have been intimidated to stop him giving evidence.

Chapter 24

CHIEF INSPECTOR MASTERS WAS in a foul mood, as he left HQ. What right had that young big headed, self-satisfied moron of a Chief Constable had telling him that there were the beginnings of a gang war? He had even hinted that he thought that Masters was not up to it and might need help. So maybe its centre was within a few miles of Masters District. Masters already knew that, after all he was not an idiot, this thought, not held by anybody else though. Then to have to listen to the man ramble on telling him to put his best man on a job to get this gang warfare stopped at once was the biggest insult of all. Masters had read the crime reports over the last months and he had realised as well as anybody else that there must be a new gang of people moving into his area. So far this new gang seemed only interested in having a war with the low-life scum, and that was no loss to the general public. A number of quite nasty criminals had vanished off the face of the earth. As far as he was concerned, if this new gang wanted to kill members of other gangs and left Joe public alone, so what. If this new gang had the ability to takeover the crime of the whole city then once, they had beaten the other gangs into submission then the crime rate would begin to drop and he Chief Inspector Masters would naturally claimed all the credit for this. The three raids one on the police station and the other two on the army camps, now they did worry him. A group of very hard people had decided to arm themselves; first, they had tried the police station. Not finding too many weapons there, Masters believed they had then moved on to the army camps. It was not very often that Masters managed to work situations out, but this time he seemed to be ahead of the rest of the police. Now if the gang that had done the police station and army camps decided to takeover the crime, then Masters believed the police might just have more on their plate than they could manage. Still he did not think that somebody clever enough to pull off the two arms raids would be interested in the crime in this city. He really did believe that this was two separate groups of people.

Chief Inspector Masters was a career police officer; he had joined the police force at 18 years old, as a normal pc plod. Now 26 years later he was a chief inspector. He would tell people that he had risen through ranks entirely due to his ability to apprehend criminals, by working out their future movements, he would explain to people that he had a wonderful police officer's nose. He could also recite at dinner parties daring deeds whereby his single-handed ability to deal with large numbers of people; he had arrested, or been a major influence in the arrest of several major criminals. He would say that the position that he held now was due to his natural brainpower and cunning. That his natural super powers of deduction had him were he was now. Those powers would let him archive further promotion in the very near future. Chief Inspector Masters believed his own propaganda 100 per cent and he fully believed that everyone else did. The people that knew the truth about him would tell you that Chief Inspector Masters was a morally corrupt individual without any sense of shame, a man who would grab the credit for any deed that would make him look good. A man with a Teflon skin that allowed no mistakes he made stick to him. In his 26 years as a police officer, he had never managed actually to catch one Criminal all by himself. His superpowers of deduction and reasoning had set him on so many false trails and wasted so much police time that it was unbelievable, but each time he had messed up he managed to slide the blame on to someone else. He became so good at it that other police officers refused to work with him. His first promotion was to keep him off the streets and to save having to discipline good police officers for refusing to go out with him. The powers to be thought it safer for all concerned to sit him behind a desk, he had always managed to rely on his in-built ability to take the credit for anything good from the person that deserved it and claimed the credit for himself. Likewise, if it went wrong then it was never his fault. The politest nickname that he had amongst his colleagues was,

"Butt Fucker."

When he arrived back at the station he sat behind his desk still fuming at the lecture that he had from the Chief Constable.

"Put my best men on it, be fucked." There was no way that he was going to waste good men on something like this. Who ever investigated this gang if ever they could find out who they were would probably end up in hospital or worse. He could see no reason to waste good men that could be out catching real criminals and enhancing his, Chief Inspector Master's name. He began to go mentally through the detectives under his control; he had come to a stop when he reached Detective Sergeant Jim Mackle. He picked up the phone and was connected to the CID room,

"Send sergeant Mackle up." He thought Mackle would be just the man for a job; there was a side bonus as well, if anything happened to Mackle it would not matter. He could well do without sergeant Mackle.

Chapter 25

JIM MACKLE WAS WHAT most of the C I D classed as a chancer, at 33 years old he had been a detective sergeant for three years, in his career as a policeman he had won three awards for bravery. The first was diving into a nearly frozen river to rescue two small children and their mother from a car that had skidded out of control and gone into the river.

The second was for facing down a cornered teenager with a pistol at the end of a very badly run attempt to rob an off-licence. What Jim Mackle never told anybody about that incident was the fact that the light was shining on the cylinder of the pistol and he could see that there was nothing loaded in any of the chambers?

The third award for bravery was when he gave himself as a hostage in a bank raid in exchange for a group of women and children. That third time was when he was promoted to sergeant and posted to the station controlled by Masters. Up until then Jim had been a dedicated police officer although most of the CID members cast him as a bit of a chancer. Within a few days of having joined the station, Jim managed to arrest two very prominent men in the car ringing business. As a reprisal, a couple of the gang of car ringers managed to corner Jim and he received a bad beating that ended up with him in hospital for over a week. Meanwhile Chief Inspector Masters managed to take all the credit for the operation and make it look as if Jim's involvement had been by accident.

Three months later, he came home to discover that his wife had run off with a young lad from one of the supermarkets. She left him a note saying that she could no longer stand worrying whether he was going to come home in a bad mood because of this Masters fellow had stitched him up yet again, or whether he would be in hospital or worse still even dead. She was going to opt for a nice comfortable safe life with the chap from the supermarket.

It was at this point that Jim Mackle started to believe that maybe the criminals might have the right idea. Take what you want when you want it. With this new attitude, Jim in the last year had been before two disciplinary boards, his ability as a thief taker had considerably reduced, and he was currently under investigation due to the loss of a large amount of money and two kilos of drugs that had been recovered after the arrest of a small local gang.

He sat in front of Masters, with the attitude-running round in his head that if Masters said the wrong word then he would tell him to stick his job. There was no way that they could prove that he had the money or the drugs in fact he didn't have the drugs he had sold them the day that they went missing. Now in an offshore bank account that would take a lot of finding he had £96,000 towards his retirement funds. Masters had opened the conversation by offering Jim a large whisky, this sent Jims mind spinning this was not something that he was expecting.

"Jim I have got what I think might be a really interesting case for you. I have the feeling than a new gang has started to operate in this area, as far as I can work out for now they seem to be concentrating on taking over the other gangs. I want you to go through the files and pick out any cases that look like they are anything to do with this new game. You can then reopen any investigation that you might think fit, but find this gang for me. We cannot have people doing what they like on our patch. You will be answerable directly to me. There is no reason for you to involve anyone else, or tell them what you are doing. Let's keep this between you and I." Mackle nodded.

"You're giving me an open brief to track down this gang?" Masters agreed,

"You will be by yourself on this case as I cannot afford to give you any help." Mackle thought to himself

"Yes and if I find them you will grab the all credit you bastard." Mackle left the office and started to think that maybe he could turn this gang to his advantage all sorts of possibilities were tumbling through his mind.

Chapter 26

J IM M ACKLE HAD BEEN through the files and he had come up with a list of crimes that his brains and intuition if not the facts told him that there could possibly be a link.

The first one was the death of a gang boss and his wife. Put down as a burglary that went wrong. It just did not sit right with Jim. It had been set up with just enough details so that any lazy police officer that was looking for an easy out could put it down to a petty burglary that had gone wrong. Fair enough, the house had been ransacked and the safe was empty. The gang boss's wife had been raped and had her throat cut. The gang boss, Alberto executed, forced to his knees and then shot once right between the eyes from a very close range. Because his safe had been opened and it had a combination lock showed that the intruders had already got that open. That it probably contained money and possibly jewels was certain, which is what they would have been wanting. He could understand that maybe the woman had been assaulted as a means of making Alberto give over the combination. It takes a lot of courage or total indifference for one man to kill another human, so after getting the contents of the safe, which had been opened at the beginning of the raid because Alberto and his wife appeared to have been in the lounge when the intruders came into the house. Why was the house really ransacked, or made to look that way? There would be a lot of money in that safe, it just didn't sit right that an intruder or intruders would come into the house tie up Alberto's wife raped her and kill her, empty the safe then kills Alberto and then ransacked the house for trinkets. It was very strange that no jewellery had turned up. The more he looked at the file the more Jim began to believe that Alberto was an assassination. In the language of the Americans, a contract fulfilled. Normal intruders looking for a bit of hard cash did not cut women's throats and blow men's brains out of the back of their heads. In addition, why was the burglar or burglars armed with a pistol? Burglary was mainly a crime committed by low-life criminals, most of it committed when the chance occurred most burglars wouldn't know one end of a pistol from another; OK maybe one a two of them would have a knife in their pocket, but to cut a woman's throat? The people that had fulfilled the contract had left no evidence of whom they were but thoughtfully had left the police and easy way of writing the case off. Jim sat back and chuckled to himself. If he was right this gang could end up causing Chief Inspector Masters an awful lot of trouble and maybe even his position.

The next crime that he had pulled out for extra attention was one about the deaths of a pimp and his girlfriend. At first glance, the crimes could be put down maybe as a crime of passion. The punter falling in love with the girl even though she's a prostitute, and then realising that her pimp was just after his money possibly even blackmailing him. It was feasible that the murderer planned to confront the pimp but had got into a rage and killed them both. That is exactly the way the police had read the situation on finding the bodies. Looking at the files and statements it became clear to him that one man by himself could not have killed both the people if they were in the room at the same time. Both the man and a woman killed as they sat in chairs around table. This made quite clear by the coroner in his report. Reading everything through three or four times he had concluded that although the Times of death were very close together, one of them must have died first when the other was not in the room. Now this meant that either somebody had a very lot of luck, or somebody had planned this killing down to the last seconds. Jim believed that the killing had been planned but he could find no motive for it. There was also the fact that and it strengthened Jim's idea that this was a set up killing, the prostitute that died was the one that rented the room, and when she did so she told the Landlord that it was for a private dinner party. The proprietor had joked with her about her not making any money out of that, he was well aware of the trade that she followed and he was always happy to rent the girls a room on a half hour basis. She had rented it for all night.

The third file that he kept out was the raid on a police station. This raid at first glance seemed a little bit pointless weapons could be bought on the streets of the city for a couple of hundred pounds each. The police station had been raided which in itself was a risky business, two men had been killed quite brutally and a few pistols had been stolen. Surely, somebody taking this much trouble to get weapons would have taken the rifles too, if for no other reason but to sell them. The value of the crime did not come to much more than £2,000 why would any criminal go to the extent that these people had for so little return. The planning had been immaculate; false alarm calls to the police station had all been made on unregistered pay-as-you-go mobile phones with the numbers withheld which made them untraceable. The calls themselves were obviously meant to scatter the police from the station all over the district. The raid timed to take place in the small space of time that it took reinforcements to reach a police station. This to him explained the force alarm call the day before. With the raid on the police station, there was also the death of a young prostitute that had occurred within a hundred yards of the police station. Jim was not sure if the two were connected but he had to consider the fact that they could be. The young woman had been found sitting on a park bench with her neck broken, in her handbag were the normal items of her trade, a large packet of condoms, a pack of wet wipes, four clean pairs of knickers and three used pairs, also a large bundle of money. All this pointed to the fact that she had died for reasons that did not include robbery. There was no reason for the prostitute to be in that park or even that area. Prostitutes in the City were well aware that that part of the city was a no-go area. Jim Mackle began to think that the people he was looking for were at the best very lucky, or they were very ruthless and well organised. The raid on the police station really started Jim thinking, just suppose that this gang or group whatever it was had done the police station job to demonstrate to the rest of the underworld exactly what they were capable of. Now take that one-step further; it could be a warning to the police, advising them not to look too hard for this gang.

Chapter 27

JIM SAT BACK IN his chair thinking about this gang. If this   gang carried out these three crimes and possibly, a lot more they were going to be a real force to reckon with. Now all he had was an impression of an unseen force that was about as solid as a puff of smoke.

If there was such a gang then he decided that this gang was going places and it would possibly be in his interest to find out who they were, what they were planning to do and possibly join them. He could see that his loyalty to the police had faded, thanks to Inspector Masters; he could also see that these people could use somebody like him to keep the police even further away from them.

At first, Jim found information very hard to obtain from his informants. They knew nothing, or for some reason they were not telling him anything. After some very heavy threats and quite a lot of money, Jim gradually managed to get little snippets of information. This new gang was calling itself the Guild, and was building itself such a reputation that even the greediest of informants was terrified that anything they said about the Guild would get back to the members. The Guild only had one punishment for every crime "Death." It turned out, from what he could piece together that the Guild had moved into the city and put themselves up for hire for any type of criminal activity especially assassinations. In the short time they had been in the City the Guild had acquired the reputation of being true to their word, any job undertaken by them carried out in such a manner that there was no argument. The Guilds reputation was so fearsome that even the most hardened criminals in the city were in no rush to cross them. The information that came to Jim about the Guild came mostly as rumour not fact, hearing it piece by piece. Jim started to put together a better picture of the Guild. They were a very close-knit group of people who were so ruthless that they seem to have no regard for a human life.

For months now, Jim had been looking for a way to make lots of money even if it meant turning against his comrades in the police force. The only thing that really stopped him becoming an out and out criminal was the threat of time in jail. An ex police officer in a jail surrounded by people that he had personally arrested was not something that Jim really fancied. The more he found out about the Guild the more he started to think that these people had the right idea and the thought of joining the Guild started to become a priority with him. He had heard unbelievable rumours about an initiation test to join the Guild; apparently, the new member would have to kill somebody in front of witnesses who were members of the Guild. Jim realise that once this was done there was no way that that person could give evidence against another member of the Guild. On first thoughts, Jim had thought that maybe he could infiltrate this group, but then as he thought about it he began to realise that maybe this was something that he had really been looking for, for a long time.

After a lot, more probing and many more threats he managed to find out that Jake was one of the top people in the Guild. Jim then spent the next few days working out what he should do and how he should do it. In the end, he decided that if it were possible he would join the Guild but not on behalf of the police. He would join them for his own benefits; it was time he made some money. He also decided that from the information he had received the Guild played things straight. He would stand a better chance if he presented himself without embellishment or hiding the fact that he was a police officer. It was a big step for Jim he had done a few dodgy things in his time but he had never killed anybody in cold blood but he did believe that he was capable of it, it was such a large commitment that he had to make sure in his own mind that the price was right.

Chapter 28

IT TOOK ALL THE bottle that Jim had to approach Jake, he had found Jake by sheer luck, he had gone into the blue feathers for a quiet drink he was very surprised to see one of his informants drinking at the bar.

"Not your normal pub is it?" he said as he stood at the bar next to him. The informant a small mean-looking man in his late Fifties nearly dropped his drink.

"I'm waiting for a mate and I don't need to be seen talking to you not with him in the pub." As he said this, he tossed his head backwards indicating a large bald-headed man sat at one of the tables at the back of the room.

"You've been asking too many questions about Jake and if he sees you and me together he will probably kill me so why don't you fuck off and leave me alone?" Jim nodded took his drink and sat down at an empty table. As far as he could see Jake hadn't taken the slightest bit of notice of him. After about 10 minutes, Jim went back to the bar got two pints of beer, walked to Jakes table and sat down. Jakes cold hard eyes stared at him without any sign of interest.

"What do you want?" Jim had to concentrate hard to make his voice sound normal.

"First things first, I want no misunderstanding, I pose no threat to you or your friends. I am a police officer; in fact I am a detective sergeant with the local CID." With that he showed Jake his warrant card.

"I will not waste your valuable time I know quite a lot about the Guild and I would like to join." He them put a card on the table with his phone number on it.

"Talk to your companions, my phone number is on that card if they want to get in touch with me they can. I think I could be very useful for your people. If my information is right I do understand what initiation fees are involved, the fact that I'm willing to undertake them should show you how serious I am," With that he finished his drink and left. Outside he had to lean against a wall to stop from shaking and it was all we could do to keep the contents of his stomach in his stomach.

Jim received a phone call from Jake instructing him to be at the blue feather at 11:30 am in four days' time. He was to have £5,000 in used notes with him. At 11.30 Jim Mackle was sat in the blue feather drinking a pint of lager he did not know it at the time that two of the men in the crowded bar had been studying him for the last 10 minutes. Six normal members of the Guild were also in the bar each of them carrying two pistols. Rab and Max along with the six other members were all in the bar by 10.30 watching to make sure that Jake wasn't being set up and also there to offer Jake back-up should anything go wrong. Such were the Guilds belief now that captured by the forces of law and order was not an option. If there was any trouble, they were quite prepared to shoot their way out with not one single thought on how many people might die. They had watched Jim walk in and buy a pint and sit down nobody had been near him apart from the barman when he had ordered his drink, he had spoken to nobody else. Jake walked into the bar, paying no attention to Jim he went to the bar, slowly sipping his pint Jake scanned the room in a mirror behind the bar until his eyes met Max. Max rubbed the end of his nose as if he had an itch. This a pre-arranged signals, telling Jake that as far as Max could see there was no trap. Jake turned round facing the room and looked directly at Jim. He finished his pint and walked into the gents.

As Jim entered the gents he was grabbed by Jake spun round facing a wall Jake kicked his legs apart and frisked him just like the American coppers do in the movies. He was looking for any means of communication making sure that Jim was clear of weapons or recording devices. All we found was Jim's mobile, which he removed the battery from, then he put it back in Jim's pocket. In the top of Jim's left boot Jake found a small double-edged knife with a knuckle-duster for a handle,

"What the fucking hell is this little thing?" Jim turned to face him and with a large grin said,

"That my friend is Detective Sergeant Jim Mackie's private personal back-up system." Jack gave him the knife back, "Point taken, we all need a friend now and again." They both went back into the bar and sat at a table drinking another pint of beer.

"I take it that the decision has been in my favour?" Jake raised one eyebrow,

"What makes you so confident that it has?" Jim grinned, "Well I reckon it's down to one of two things Jake, it's either my wonderful coppers nose for ferreting out information, or it's a fact I was told to bring £5,000 along." With that, he pulled out a package from his inside pocket and gave it to Jake. Jake had felt it in Jim's pocket when the searched him, he left it there knowing what it contained. Jake left it on the table for the moment and nodded.

"If you shape up then you are in, but be aware, if you don't shape up then you'll be dead, those are our terms. I understand that you have no real evidence against the Guild and I don't trust you as far as I can spit an elephant. You are being invited to join against my better judgment, if I can make you back out before it goes too far then I'll be happy." Jim looked at Jake and in a firm strong voice said,

"Jake you've been in trouble with the law for years; I quite understand that like most criminals you have a natural dislike for people like me. Just remember the feeling is mutual, but I have turned up at a meeting with you and put £5,000 on a table and am about to kill someone. Can you not understand that by doing this I am making a complete unchangeable act and in crossing over the tracks, there is no possible way that after today I can go back to the life that I have been leading. You will just have to learn to trust me. There is no way that I intend to back down now, in fact I've gone too far already it is not possible for me to back down." Jake studied the man and he started to realise that what the man was saying had a ring of truth in it.

"We will see about that! At 2 am tonight, you will be in a phone box outside the bingo hall and I did say at 2 am not 1:55 am. You will find a small package by the directors in that packet you will find a mobile phone, at five minuets past 2 the phone will ring and you be given directions. Be there." With that, Jake got up and as he stood, he picked up the package with the £5,000 and it. On his way out, he walked past Rab who sat at a table and without Jim, seeing pasted the package to him. Then he walked out of the pub. Jake walked about the city for the next 20 minutes making sure he was not being followed meanwhile Rab and Max followed Jim back to his house.

At 1:45 am, Jake put the package with the mobile phone in a phone box and melted back into the shadow of an alleyway. Two am precisely Jim's car stopped outside the phone box, Jim retrieve the packet and opened it. Jim had no sooner picked up the phone than it rang He had taken it for granted that either Jake or one of the others would be watching him from a vantage point, they would not take him on trust.

"Where am I going?" Jim was feeling rather nervous; the voice on the phone was Jakes even though he was trying to disguise it.

"Drive your car about 300 yards down the road and park underneath a lamp-post that is not working, leave this phone on." Jim did as he told and once parked up Jakes voice came back on the phone.

"Step out of you car, stand on the pavement." Again Jim did as he was told.

"Now do exactly as you are told. Take every bit of clothing off and put it all on the front seat of your car."

"You must be fucking mad, what do you want, a fucking peepshow?" Although he did not like the idea, once again Jim did as told.

"Leave the phone with the clothes, lock the car and put the keys on top of the front nearside wheel. When you have done that, cross the road to the car that is opposite you. On the front seat, you will find a set of overalls and a set of trainers, put them on. Get in the car and drive it to the back of the Comet warehouse on the industrial estate do it now and make sure you do not take any detours. I will contact you when you are needed." With that the phone went dead Jim drove the car to the back of a warehouse as instructive. He kept his eyes open for anybody following him but could seen nobody, this was making him very uneasy as he could not understand how they were going to see and control what he was doing. It flashed into his mind that maybe he had been lured into a lonely area to be disposed of, maybe this Guild had decided that it was easier to kill him than it was to trust him. As he pulled up at the back of a warehouse, Jake raised himself from the back seat of the car.

"You're doing well so far make sure you keep it up." This surprise nearly caused him to faint he had had no idea that Jake was in the car. Jims respect for the way this Guild was working was growing by the minute. So far he could not see how they had put a foot wrong, if he had been trying to entrap them, there was no way that he could give concrete evidence of what had happened so far. Unless he had, a tape recorder stuck up his backside there was no way he could have recorded or relayed any of the instructions to anybody else.

"Get out of the car." Jake still really did not trust Jim and it showed in the way he was acting.

"You get one chance at this and that is all, if you cock it up I will kill you. This is your last chance to back away without any sort of reprisals." Jim looked him squarely in the eyes and taking a deep breath to steady his nerves.

"I want in." Jake nodded; maybe just maybe he was beginning to feel a little bit of respect for Jim Mackle.

"OK you follow me and do exactly as you are told." They walked to the edge of a building and remaining in the shadows they could see on the other side of the road a police car with two police officers sitting in the front seats. Apparently, this was a regular parking space for these two police officers. They were obviously taking a coffee break as one poured the coffee from a flask into two cups, the other was unwrapping a packet of sandwiches. The police car was sat nicely under a street lamp, which gave a good few of both police officers in the front seats.

"How do I kill one and not the other?" It appeared that his victim was going to be a police officer.

"You don't kill one you will kill both of them. Killing two police officers is your entrant's fee." Jake replied.

It was then that Jim noticed that Jake was wearing thin rubber gloves. Jake handed him a 9 mm Browning semi-automatic pistol

"There are four live rounds in the magazine to prime the weapon you pull the slide back that puts the first round in the chamber. The safety catches off; all you will need to do is press the trigger each time you wish to fire a shot. Prime the weapon now." Jim took the weapon and primed it as told. He could not help noticing, and neither could Jake that his hands were trembling. Jake continued as if he was teaching somebody to do a simple task.

"You will approach a police car from the passenger side." Jim listened to all the instructions nodding his head to show that he understood. He started towards the car and as he did so, it went through his mind that, it was the Guild that had robbed the army camp. That was something he had wondered about when he was looking through all the crime reports. The two policemen were enjoying their coffee and sandwiches when one of them, the driver noticed in his rear-view mirror than a man was approaching from across a road the fact that the man was wearing overalls confused him for moment but then he realise that it was sergeant Mackle.

"I wonder what that renegades doing here? I didn't expect to see Mackle in overalls did you?" As Jim reached the car the police officer in the passenger seat slid down the window. "What are you doing here Jim? Don't tell me you've got a part-time job as a night watchman." Jim did not say anything instead; he bought the pistol up level with the side of a man's head and pulled the trigger. Jim felt the recall of the gun in his hand, the bullet tore through the base of the mans skull and came out just above his right ear, blood and brain splattered all over the head and shoulders of the driver as the bullet carried on and shattered the front screen of the car. As the man fell over into the driver's lap Jim gritted his teeth and shot the driver through the chest Jake quietly walked up to the car and focused a video camera on the driver's face then he drew back until he got Jim and the driver in focus.

"This one is not dead Jim put one right between his eyes when I tell you to." James hand was shaking but he did as he told at the word from Jake he pressed the trigger for the third time. Even in the still night, the sound of shots sounded no louder than a car backfiring and even if they had this was a deserted industrial estate with nobody else there to hear them. As a third, shot rang out the back of man's head exploded into the headrest blood, brains and gristle all over the back of a car. Jake moved round so that he had a clear view of Jim as he fire the fourth and final round into the already dead police officers in the passenger seat. Jake held out a clear polythene bag,

"Put the gun in the bag Jim." Jim had a vacant stare on his face his hands were shaking and he felt as if he was about to throw up. He managed to control himself as he dropped the gun into the bag.

"Now you have to understand that I am genuine Jake? I have fully committed myself and I now know there is no turning back. Even if I was to give evidence against the Guild there is no court in the land that would pardon me for this act, is there?" Finally Jake held out his hand and said,

"Welcome to the Guild Jim Mackle." Jim drove the car back to where he had left his own, once again, he stripped off and then redressed himself in his own clothes, the overalls trainers and phone placed into a bag and Jake told him it was up to him to dispose of them.

As he drove away, he looked in his rear-view mirror and at first; he could just see a small flicker of flame, which suddenly blossomed into a fireball. Jake had destroyed the other car to remove any sort of evidence.

The next morning Jake was behind his desk in the CID office, the panda with the two dead police officers had been discovered about 7 o'clock that morning and all CID officers had been recalled into the station. The station was in deep shock and anger at the death of their two comrades. The very fact that police officers gunned down in sheer cold blood for no apparent reason had everybody hopping mad. The officers obviously had not pulled anybody over for questioning because of the coffee and sandwiches that were in their laps when found. There was no sign of a break-in at any of the factories or warehouses on the estate. There was just no reason for the crime. There was also no real evidence except for the spent bullets and cases recovered by forensic officers. These bullets could not be matcher to any weapon that the police had on file. The bullets were 9 mm, which led the police to believe that the weapon came from the army. Jim made a show of phoning his informants trying to get any sort of information. In truth, he was still in shock from the night before. He had never killed anybody before and as soon as he got home, he sat on the toilet with the runs while being sick in the sink. He had always known that he had a violent streak in him, but he had never realised before that he would get such enjoyment and such a rush of adrenalin from killing another person. He had to admit to himself that now the shock had worn off he would be quite happy to kill again. When he thought nobody was looking he pulled back his watch and looked at the small number three tattooed on the back of his left wrist, He was now a fully-fledged member of what was probably the most ruthless organisation that had ever surfaced in this country. He had the feeling that from now on, his life was going to undergo a complete change and he could only see it getting better. He gathered all his notes concerning the Guild and put them through the shredder. He then sat down to complete a document describing a small bunch of petty criminals that had individually committed crimes, which were really outside their league. It was not brilliant but it would do to keep Chief Inspector Masters out of his hair for a while.

Chapter 29

MAX, RAB AND JAKE decided that it was time to take stock of what they had done so far,

"I have nothing against killing," Rab said,

"Although so far it has bought us money I can't see us make our fortunes out of just killing people."

The other two nodded in agreement.

"People don't really trust us enough to hire us." This was from Jake. Jake had taken to the idea of the Guild so well that he was starting to show quite a good ability at handling people.

"I have been thinking about that" Max voice was very quiet and he had a gleam in his eyes, when he told the other two that he had an answer to their problems.

"So far and we have quite a few members and a lot of cash let us keep recruiting members after all we don't want to do all the work our ourselves do we? In addition, the lump sums of each new member keep us in cigarettes and beer. Let us keep the contract business going but also let us make a few changes. When I initiated Sally to the Guild, I told her; with our assistance and guidance she would take over all the massage parlours, prostitutes and pimps in fact all the sex industry in this City. If we set up each of our members to control different aspects of crime in this city then we three can claimed a percentage from the top of each business. We will have to fight to takeover each of the main gangs that control the crime in this city. There are a lot of different gangs so many of them will not like what we intend to do. Given the choice between us running their business with them still making a good living or being dead, then I think they will choose us. The reputation that we have now will go a long way to help them make up their minds. I also think that when a chance arises we should choose a demonstration of how we deal with people that upset us personally. There is this to remember that once we climb to the top of the pile, then we must stay there, we cannot afford to give an inch. Doing it this way we only need to keep our members from prison or any other sort of trouble. Our members with luck should not come to the attention of the public. People that we control must be in mortal fear of us and we must instil in the outsiders, the normal people that are working for the other gangs, or protected by them that we have a rigid code of silence. The very fact that Jim Mackle managed to find us means that the normal informants are not frightened enough of us to keep silent. We need to be so ruthless that nobody utters a word against us and it must never enter into his or her minds to give evidence against us. Jake and Rab sat drinking their whiskeys, thinking over what Max had said. It all seemed to make a lot of sense to them after all there was a lot of money moving from innocent and normal Joe public type of people into the pockets and a bank accounts of so many different criminal types of people. If the Guild stepped in at the right place then the local thugs would still get all the blame for the crime and the Guild would skim money off the top and still be unknown to Joe public. Each member of the Guild had been tested and found to be true. The Guild was now fully armed and the three Grandmasters decided that they were a position to takeover the city.

Chapter 30

"I HAVE A PROBLEM," said Rab,

"We have a lot of money stashed away, not only is it not earning us any interest but it is beginning to be a bit of a liability just lying around in my room. In addition, we do need to keep some sort of paperwork so that we know who is paid what and by whom. There is also the fact that we now have 35 video tapes all showing somebody being killed. If they should ever fall into the wrong hands that would mean the end of us three. We need some safe storage for the paperwork and these films also; we seriously need to think about investing some of the money. We just do not need that amount of cash lying around. Just think what would happen if the police managed to turn up with a search warrant? In addition, we have so much money lying around, but should anybody investigates the three of us we have no means of proving how we get our income. Just remember Al Capone one of the clever gangsters, he ended up in jail for tax evasion. We have got to steer our way around that sort of problem." Max and Jake both agreed that Rab was right, in what he was saying.

"What do you suggest?" This was something that Max had not really thought about, but it did make sense. They decided that they would spend some of the money on a genuine legitimate business. Straight people could run this, but Rab would control the books, that way they could launder the money from the Guild by putting it through the books. They could be silent partners in the business thus proving their income should the need arise. After many difference suggestions, it was decided that they would buy a photographic studio; with that sort of business fictitious customers could pay large amounts of money for wedding photos, family portraits and other sorts of photographic artwork. Because it would all be digital there would be no need for a long paper trail. The equipment, photographic paper and all the other running expenses could well be legitimate. This solution to the storage of the video tapes and normal everyday accounts for the Guild was to buy a small-detached house on the outskirts of the city and converted to their purposes. This was left to Max because of his very inventive mind.

Chapter 31

MAX SPENT A LOT of time thinking about the security of the group. At last, he came up with the beginnings of an idea. He remembered a conversation he had had one day with a fellow inmate when he was in prison. The man was Polish and he had been telling Max about the small village that he came from in Poland. He kept going on about the wonderful trades people that could be found there, plumbers, builders, electricians, plasterers plus any sort of trade you could think of he had told Max that nearly everybody in the village was capable of first class work as it was in their upbringing.

Using one of the younger members of the Guild and one of Sally's pretty prostitutes Max went on a tour of the estate agents, to all intents and purposes, it looked as if an indulgent father was trying to find a house for his daughter and her future husband. Eventually Max settled on a detached house just on the edge of the city, this was a three-bedroom house in about a quarter of an acre of ground. A high wall surrounded the house with no neighbours over looking it. The house duly purchased and paid for. The day after the sale was completed Max flew out to Poland. When he returned to England, he had six good tradesmen with him. As arranged, Jake met them at the airport; he was driving a large van, with no windows. From the inside rear of the van nobody could see through the windscreen because of a fitted wooden partition. Once the Polish tradesmen were in the back of the van Jake drove round for about two and a half hours before setting off to the new house. There was no way that the Poles would know where they were. On reaching the house, Jake backed the van right up to the front door and the men were hustled straight into the house. All the windows had been blacked out so that nobody could see what the men would be doing; also, there was no chance of the men recognising anything of the local area. Officially, the men were on three weeks' holiday to England to see the sights. In reality paid very good money to come to England. They were to carry out many alterations to the Guilds house. After that, they would be flown home to Poland. No matter how the men were questioned, they had been taken from the airport straight into a blacked-out house they had seen no countryside no town names, and they had no idea where they were or had been.

The house had a large pantry next to the kitchen. This made into two small rooms. The entrance to one of them was a large safe door set into the wall instead of a normal door. This then could be classed as a security door. The idea being that this would make a legitimate gun storeroom. In the name that he had used to buy the house Max had applied for a shotgun licence, he had brought four shotguns and he would chain them to a rack in this room. After it had been finished the police actually congratulated Max on the security of these weapons. The floor of the gunroom dug out and three large rooms, a toilet and shower unit formed underneath. Air events were built naturally they were concealed. Running water, heating and Electric also added was kitchen. In fact, a complete suit of rooms although rather small was beneath the house. Max had now made a complete secured area for Rab to keep his paperwork and the video tapes of the initiation films. The house was naturally fitted with a very expensive and intensive burglar alarm system and incorporated into that, one could by tapping in the right code open a small panel in the gunroom. A remote control pointed at this panel would cause the floor to slide back revealing a set of stairs that led down to the underground rooms. Once down there the floor slid back and anybody entering the gunroom would find nothing out of place. The house was then decorated top-to-bottom and to an outsider an indulgent father had given a nice house to his young daughter and her partner.

A month later rumour went round that the young couple had both died in a motoring accident whilst on honeymoon. The distraught father then rented the house out to a young executive. Naturally, he was a member of the Guild. A timing system worked out that more-or-less allowed Rab access to these rooms whenever he needed.

Chapter 32

Rab sat in his office in the safe house, he called it a safe house, the other two Grandmasters and the three Sub Masters all called it Rabs rabbit hole. As he thought of it, a small smile appeared on his face. How his life had changed, from being banged up in prison, to one of the three main men that were taking over a whole city. Once the safe house was finished, Rab decided that it was time that he set about putting the finances of the Guild into action. They had bought a small photographic studio, that employed a photographer and a receptionist, and apart from the money, that Rab was running through the books the business was really doing quite well. Rab had started spreading the tentacles of the Guild through the city. While Max and Jake concentrated on taking over different groups of criminals, Rab concentrated his mind to making the best use of what they had achieved. He found a medium-sized backstreet garage that was steadily going out of business; he approached the owner with the idea that with an injection of cash the garage could continue trading. A partnership was formed between the garage owner and one of the members of the Guild that had taken over quite a large gang of car thieves. The owner of the garage put up the deeds to the property and the Guild and put up a lump of money. With new equipment, the garage started to thrive a little bit. Them, unfortunately after about a month the owner of the garage while road testing a car was involved in a serious accident caused by a young lad in a stolen car. The young lad had managed to get out and leg it, but the garage owner was very badly damaged, in fact after three months in hospital the poor man died. This then left the Guild with a nice backstreet garage where cars that had been stolen could be either stripped down for spare parts or be fitted with false number plates, VIN number's and sold on elsewhere. Cars were cut and shut and a real thriving business emerged from this run-down backstreet garage. Next, a scrap yard that was run by quite a hard gang decided after a few accidents and the death of one of its leaders that maybe it would be better to be protected by the Guild. The protection was very reasonable 10 percent of the takings plus full control over the books. Cars stripped for second hand parts used in the garage, the rest sold to the normal punters; also, a scrap yard is very handy for getting rid of any vehicles looked for by the police.

A small machines shop was then added to the list again a deal was struck with the owner, who as soon has he got an inkling of what was happening decided that he would rather go abroad and live as a silent partner. The machine shop was quite a nice business with plenty of work. There was always time to make tools for different members of the Guild, such as lock picks, breaking and entry tools, and of course, when you needed to strengthen the front of a motor for ram-raid the machine shop was ideal place to make the strengthening bars for the front, then fitted at the garage.

After the machine shop, came general wholesalers. This had come in very handy for getting rid of good stolen goods from factories.

As the money came rolling in a few second-hand shops were taken over so the groups that had been taken over by the Guild would stand less risk when they come to sell their stolen goods. It was decided to take on a couple of extra legitimate businesses. The businesses that Rab chose were a florist and a bakery both of these had a high amount of wasted stock so it was quite easy to lose quite a lot of money through paperwork. The Guild was expanding at such a rate that it was all Rab could do to keep up with the paperwork never mind go out and experience once again the thrill and the adrenalin rush of what the rest of the Guild was doing. Rab was happy to sit in his rabbit hole, after all figures and books were his lively hood, but he had to admit that he did miss the rush of seeing somebody absolutely terrified of what he was going to do next.

Chapter 33

8:00 PM ON A Wednesday evening and the bar was full of men and women out for a quiet midweek drink. Two young men in their late twenties swaggered into the bar, as they stood at the bar waiting to be served they surveyed the other people that sat at the tables.

"We will sit at that table over there with those two old men are playing dominoes." To the barman he said

"Two pints mate." when the barman put the pints of beer on the bar the two men picked them up, and started to walk away from the bar. The barman had been around a long time, he had seen hard men by the score and he had never been impressed by any of them. He had his own system for dealing with hard cases lying on the shelf under the bar was a brand new shiny ripsaw; whenever there was trouble in the bar he would waive the saw in the air like a sword. Troublemakers would take one look at the wobbly bendy blade with the large teeth and decide that maybe they did not want trouble after all. Many times, men that had only had one thing on their minds and that was to cause damage to somebody else and to the room all of a sudden changed their minds. The rip saw really did make a fearsome weapon, Design to saw along the grain of wood the saw had large off set teeth, and being long and quite heavy was capable of causing the most ghastly gashes and of course it was possible to actually take someone's arm off with it. As the barman spoke, his hand came to rest on the handle of the saw.

"Excuse be gentlemen but you seem to have accidentally forgotten to pay for your beers." Both of the young men swaggered back to the barn and put their beers on the bar. One of them moved his watch up his arm to show what looked like a number three tattooed on the back of his wrist,

"I didn't quite hear what you said old man." The barman let go of the saw handle

"I'm sorry gentlemen it was an honest mistake I did not know who you were. It will never happen again and the drinks are naturally on the house." The young man looked at him and with a wink at his mate he said

"Unless you want a lot of trouble, make sure it never does. We'll let it go this time, just remember who you are talking to next time and as sign of goodwill we will have two of those large cigars." The two young men then swaggered over to the table where to old pensioners were playing dominoes. Leaning down one of the young men pushed the dominoes off the table and on to the floor.

"What is it going to be, that is the question, do you move to another table or do you spend the rest of your miserable lives in wheelchairs. Make up your minds quickly we wish to sit down." The two old men reluctantly picked up their dominoes and moved to another table. The two young men sat down with large grins on their faces.

"Barman I think we'll have some food when you are ready". The barman had only ever met one member of the Guild. That was when his boss, had decided it was better to pay protection, or as the man from the Guild put it "Insurance." His boss had told him that any man or woman identify themselves, by showing the figure three in black tattooed on the back of their left wrist were given whatever hospitality they would ask for. The trouble was the fact that the barman saw the tattoo on the young man's wrist written in black Biro. The barman also understood that to upset a member of the Guild could bring about instant violence so great that even his ripsaw would not be able to handle it, and afterwards the Guild would extract such a heavy penalty for his boss that he would probably lose his job.

As all this was happening, nobody took any notice of a rather scruffy man sat at a corner table reading his newspaper, after the two men sat down the scruffy man walked into the gent's toilet. The phone call that he made bought two more men into the bar, Max and Jake. Jake sat down at a table while Max went to the bar and brought the drinks. On his way back from the bar to the table Max nodded to the scruffy man, the man picked up his drink and as he took a sip, his eyes pointed Max to the two men with the tattoos. Max and Jake sat drinking their beers just like any normal everyday punters, when Jakes glass was empty, he stood up, said goodbye to Max and then walked out of the bar. 20 minutes later the two young men got up to leave on their way past the barman one of them said,

"£50 should cover a taxi fare." The barman went to the till and handed over the money. The two men said nothing else and walked out of the bar. Outside the one with the money said to his partner,

"I told you it would be easy, people are so shit scared of this fucking Guild that a black number three under your watch will get you anything that you ask for. Let's go downtown to one of the massage parlours, the Guild fucks so many people we may as well have a free fuck on them." Two men stepped out from the shadows of a shop doorway, and blocked the path in front of the two young men. One of the young men said,

"Think again chaps. You could be biting off more than you think." With that, he pulled back his watch to show the black number three on his wrist. The two men blocking the path did not bat an eyelid; the larger of the two looked at the young men and in a quiet voice said

"I've got a tattoo like that, your only problem is I earned mine and this tattoo is not a Biro mark." With that, he pulled back his watch and showed a black three tattoo. The two young men spun round and started running they did not get very far as two more men emerge from the shadow of a shop doorway blocking their path yet again. A large car pulled up beside the two young men and they were quickly bundled into the back of it. The whole operation had taken less than 30 seconds and in that part of town even if somebody had seen it and realise what was happening, nobody would have interfered. The two young men squashed together on the back seat to the car were shaking with fear. They both knew that by impersonating Guild members and worse of all caught doing it they were a lot of trouble. The trouble is they did not realise how much trouble. What had started out as a bit of a laugh was surely going to end in tears! The two young men stammered out apologises and promised never to do anything like this again, they even offered to pay for the drinks and food that they had, with trembling hands one of the young men handed back the 50 pound but no one else in the car said a word.

Chapter 34

BERNARD HAD A MEETING with the three Grandmasters; the Guild hierarchy were now living and dressing more in line with the money that they were earning. The meeting instead of being in a backstreet pub was now in the lounge bar of quite a posh hotel. The drinks ordered, and the small talk carried on until the waiter had served them and left their table.

"A few weeks ago a matter of discipline was bought up, it was decided that we needed to show the informers and general scum of this city that we wouldn't stand for people talking about us in the wrong places and we needed something to put the temptation of grassing us up out of their little minds. If you think it's worth the risk I think I might have a solution to a lot of our problems on the discipline front." The three grandmasters looked at Bernard and then at each other wondering what he would come out with next.

"Go ahead Bernard."

"I met up with Bill Watson an old lag that I have known for donkey's years; he has always been a night worker. I think he has actually spent more of his adult life in jail than he has out of it. We had a few drinks and got talking about things in general. He is one of the proper old-fashioned burglars, when he is in a house if he opens a draw and it contains women's personal bits, he shuts that draw without touching anything in it. He does not wreck a house as he searches it, he says it is bad enough been burgled you do not want your personal belongings thrown all over the floor or damaged just for the fun and it. He and his wife have been married for over 35 years. His wife has stood by him every time he went into prison and waited for him, never once reproaching him for what he did, and never once being unfaithful to him.

It turns out that he has lung cancer, when it was diagnosed; they gave him three months to live. He finally told me that so far he is two months and three weeks into that three months and he still has not found the courage to tell his wife. After all these years, the money that he has put away for a rainy day totals £350. He's worrying himself witless over how his wife will cope with no money coming in."

"Very touching, but how does that affect us? We are not in the business of giving old lags handouts, especially when they're not even members of our Guild." Max and Jake agreed to what Rab had said.

"I understand that and that isn't what I'm about to suggest. We need to convince the criminal element of this city that even talking to the wrong people about us would invoke a dire punishment. Bill only has a week to live, and he would like a large wedge of money for his wife. By a large wedge, he is talking £20,000. Along with that amount of money he would like a quick death rather than the pain that he has now and the extra pain he is about to suffer. We could pay him to act as an informer against us and we could very publicly kill him. He would get his clean fast death and his wife would have £20,000 to help her survive." The other three looked at him in amazement. Max said

"What a brilliant idea, with what we've got planned for those two blokes that impersonated Guild members we could really put the Guild on the map.

They sat in a hotel lounge making their plans for the next few hours, what they were planning were so diabolical. It would put the fear of the devil in the criminal element of the city; nobody would ever dare do anything against the Guild. The police would not know or even understand what had hit them or the City. The Guild was now on the very brink of taking over the entire city. It was unbelievable that of all the deaths that had already occurred and all the deaths that would occur in the very near future were the results of a paedophile group killing one man's grandchildren.

Chapter 35

THE GUILD USED THREE large cars to ferry people to an abandoned warehouse on the edge of the city. These men were all either gang leaders and their main bodyguards, or high ranking men in different gangs. These men had not been invited they had simply been told to get into the car and keep their mouths shut. As the last car dropped off its passengers at the Warehouse doors, the passengers were ushered into a small side room. Here they were told to strip right down to nothing, the fact that three hooded men all armed with SMGs were watching them made them act quickly. Gradually the room filled, then the doors were closed and locked it was now 10:30 pm inside 60 very worried men stood about, not daring to say a word to each other as they had been told to keep their mouths shut. Such was the power of the Guild that not one man had the courage to disobey an order from a Guild member. The Guild had decided it was time to introduce themselves properly to the gangland fraternity of the city. It was known that the Guild was taking over some of the activities, now was time for the Guild to show that they intended to take over all of the activities. After today's demonstration, the takeover would be much simpler. These naked men would know that when a member of the Guild spoke no matter what he said he was to be taken seriously. The Guild had decided that the two young men, who had posed as Guild members be used as an example of the Guilds way of punishing wrong doers. That way when they visited the new establishments that they wished to offer protection to, or take over, they would have no trouble convincing the owners of exactly what they are capable of doing.

The warehouse had been deserted for quite a while, most of the windows were broken but they had all been covered with black cloth, any noise coming from the warehouse would not be heard because there was not another building within 400 yards of it. At one end of the warehouse a wooden frame had been constructed of six wooden bars tied together to make two "A" frames these two "A" frames were them placed next to each other and secured to a large beam the run across the roof of the warehouse. From each frame there were two ropes hanging from the top and two from the bottom. Four hooded men walked into the warehouse from a side door each one armed with a sub-machine gun. One of the hooded men stepped forward and fired his SMG into the roof of the warehouse. The noise was deafening the sound of a shooting seemed to echo round and round the warehouse the noise was horrendous everybody froze. When they were all looking at him the man started to talk.

"You have been bought here today to witness the punishment of two men that have acted against the Guild; they have gone against our principles and against our personal rules. Now, you are personally in no danger. I realise some of you are very nervous so I will say it again you are personally in no danger now. Mind you, should any information or hint of what is about to happen come into the hands of the police or the newspapers then the person or persons responsible will be hunted down and we the Guild will deal with them personally. I would advise you to watch and learn from what is about to happen, when a member of the Guild talks to you in the future you will understand the consequences of disobeying. We want you to remember; also, we want you to spread the word among your close associates of what happened here today. That you spread it word of mouth we will except, but remember nothing public. In future when you deal with any of our members, remember this fact there is no way that you will be asked to give free services or goods we will be part of your business and with a large discount we will pay for what we have. I will now leave you to watch the show." A second hooded man stepped forward and once again, the sound of machine gunfire filled the warehouse. As things went quiet, once again the second man said,

"What you are going to see will not be pleasant. I suggest you stand a little apart from each other so that if anybody spews up, the mess will go on the floor not you. You are naked not because we are kinky but to prevent any type of recording, also to protect your clothes from blood and spew." The lights in the warehouse went out leaving everybody in total darkness; slowly one by one four strong halogen lights, were turned, on illuminating each of the two frames. The two young men who had impersonated Guild members were frogmarched from outside and placed facing the two frames. Very quickly, the hooded men tied the young men's wrists and ankles to the frames. The men doing the tying turned and bowed to their captive audience as if they were assistance in a magic show. Next, they each produced a craft knife and quite calmly set about cutting the clothes away from the two men. When this was done, the two men were left spreadeagled on the wooden frames shaking with fear and whimpering. Two more men stepped forward each holding a curled up whip the end of each whip shone in the light showing that each end was steel capped. The audience made no sound, not even a murmur or a shuffling of bare feet could be heard. One hooded member of the Guild stepped forward in front of the blaze of lights he looked at the group of men, "The two men in front of you used the Guilds name to acquire free drinks and food and they also use our name to collect money from one barman. You may think that this was a minor offence, but use your imagination to work out what we would do if it had been a major offence. What they have done will not be tolerated by us and you have been bought here so that you can really understand that we do mean what we say. Once you leave here none of you will ever receive a second warning."

At a single shot the two men with the whips raised their arms and bought the first strokes down onto the backs of the two young men. As the flesh on their backs was ripped open blood flowed the two men screamed. The witnesses could not believe their eyes as the whipping continued and after about 10 strokes, both men's bowel and bladders had emptied onto the floor to mix with the puddles of blood that was forming around their feet. Blood started to spray out from the two men's backs and as the whips came away from the flesh the spread of blood had followed the lashes as they returned over the men's head to splatter on the floor behind them. By 15 strokes, most to the flesh had gone from the men's backs and bits of white bone could be seen through the red of the blood. After 20 strokes, most of the screaming had stopped and bits of bone were hanging from the side of the men's backs. By then most of the witnesses had been sick emptying their stomach contents on to the floor. A few of the ones in the front row, splattered with blood and bone and they had lost control of their bowels. The whipping stopped after 30 strokes, two hooded men stepped up to the limp hanging bodies and placed the muzzle of their nine millimetre sub-machineguns at the back of each man's head they fired one round into each man, brain bone and blood erupted through the front of the young men's faces scattering the teeth and eyeballs across the floor. The lights went out turning the warehouse into blackness. The doors opened, and then a burst of machine gun fire rattled round the warehouse again.

"Gentlemen you are free to go, remember what you have witnessed today, do not ever forget it.

Chapter 36

THE WHOLE TOWN WAS buzzing with the news of the punishment carried out by the Guild. Every so-called wise guy, con artists, robber, bank robber, in fact any one that could be described as a villain was worried, very worried. The Guild had taken hold of the city, they were now putting out so much fear that the crime rate in the City dropped drastically, and not because of the efficiency of the police but because people were worried about upsetting this "Guild". Everyone was waiting to see what the Guild would do next. After a tip-off to the police and the papers the two young men that had been beaten and then shot were found two days after their death. It was a member of the Guild that had given the tip-off, it was done on purpose and nearly one hundred per cent of the 60 men that were witness to the deaths were now terrified that the Guild might connect the tip-off to the police and papers with them. The fear that prevailed among these people soon spread to their associates, which of course made the Guilds power even greater.

The papers speculated a lot about these two deaths, one minute they thought it was a gangland killing but then they could not find anything to suggest that the two men had gangland connections. That theory dropped in favour of something else. The papers then went along the lines that these two young must have interfered with a young girl and this was the family extracting revenge on them. Friends of the young men soon dispersed this theory. The final theory that the papers came up with was the fact that the killing must have been something to do with a sexually related religious cult, and that these two men for some reason had been a sacrifice. The little known sauce of this way of thinking was started when a police officer called Jim gave a reporter the idea in a pub one night.

The police had no leads of any sort, they were totally baffled. For some reason nobody associated the holes in the roof of the warehouse with bullet-holes. The investigating officer was quite happy, under the guidance of the supervising police officer Sergeant Jim Mackle, to go along with the idea that some sort of religious group had sacrificed the two men. The case of the two dead men, was pushed to a back burner. Where Jim Mackle believed it would soon be forgotten.

Naturally, Inspector Masters took all credit for the sudden fall in the rate of crime in this city.

So far, the Guild had kept its dealings to the normal run of the mill crooks they had gradually, over the past few months built up quite a large protection racket. In fact, they were actually protecting the people that run protection rackets. They had taken over most of the clip joints, sauna and massage parlours and the running of the majority of the prostitutes this was bringing quite a large income and of course the Guild couldn't stop there. It was now getting close to the time that the Guild started muscling in on some of the other large and more active crooks in the City, They had had many meetings trying to work out which way to go next. After a lot of talking and deliberation, they had decided it was time to make the next move.

Chapter 37

BILL WATSON HAD BEEN a professional burglar all his life, his first conviction happened on his 18th birthday, and 40 years on, he was still breaking into houses and stealing anything he could find laying around. Among the other criminals Bill, was a "gentleman" crook. Compared to the new breed of criminal this made him a little bit of an oddity. Bill was an honest man, many times when he had been flush with money he had helped other criminals that were going through a bad patch. It was with much disbelief to the majority of criminals that knew him when the rumour went round that he had offered to become a Super grass against the new Guild. People that had attended the beating and death of the two men at the hands of a Guild just could not understand how stupid Bill Watson had become.

The police had had Bill dead to rights they had caught him half in and half out of a second storey window. During questioning, Bill had been told that this time he would go down for a long time. Bill put on show at begging for mercy He told them that he could not stand another prison term. The natural police officers answer,

"Give us something and maybe you won't have to go away." After a while, Bill had told them that he could give them information on the Guild that was causing all the trouble in the City. Straight away Bill was transferred to a nice cosy cell in the police station; a very pleasant meal was brought to him to keep him happy.

A large white van pulled up in front of the police station front doors, 15 men jumped out all wearing black balaclavas, black gloves, black boots and black boiler suits. They entered the police station, and with a police enforcer, smashed the lock, to open the door locked against the public. The two police officers in the reception box were immediately shot dead. The sound of small arms fire brought people out of the offices into the corridors, and three or four black-suited men immediately fired upon these people. Those that survived scurried back into their offices and jammed the doors shut. Five of the men rushed through the corridors straight down to the holding area. As the door flew, open two men stepped through and sprayed the room with 9 mm bullets. Two police officers died instantly and three more were wounded. Also killed at the same time were three men that had been arrested for drunken behaviour. Two more men quickly walked through the holding area to the cells and started opening the doors.

Bill Watson had heard the shooting and sat very calmly on the edge of his bunk waited for his door to open. The doors were being banged open men were shouting and then it was his turn, his door banged open and the large man stood facing him with a sub-machine gun. The two men looked each other straight in the eyes and Bill said

"Bernard, be quick!" Bernard held out his right hand and gripped Bill's right hand in his, with his left hand he raised his sub-machinegun put the front of the barrel to bills open mouth and pressed the trigger once. Bill dropped to the floor dead in an instant.

At the sound of Bernard's whistle, all the men in the police station fired a short burst from the sub-machine guns and backed out. The white van roared away and for a few moments, nobody in the police station dared to move.

To all intents and purposes, the Guild had silenced a potential informer. They had acted quickly and with such a devastating effect that the whole city was now trembling in fear.

Mrs Watson sat at the kitchen table, her eyes red from a day and a half crying, she had heard the postman come but as yet hadn't bothered to get up and see what had been put through the door. Nearly an hour later, she got to her feet and walked into the hall, two or three junk mail letters and one hand delivered envelope. She opened the envelope first, inside was a short note saying that a person would call at 3:00 pm that afternoon and he wished to talk to her about a bequest that Bill Watson had left for her. 3:00 pm that afternoon Bernard knocked on Mrs Watson's front door, the doors opened and Mrs Watson lead him into the front parlour. "Bill couldn't have left any sort of bequest to me, I have his bank book and apart from a few hundred Pounds he had nothing else."

"Mrs Watson, Bill spoke to me a few days ago he explained that he had lung cancer and only a week left to live, he was worried how you would survive. He came to us and offered us a deal. He would pretend to be an informant for the police if we would give you £20,000 and kill him before the cancer took its final toll on him." With that, Bernard put down a package on the table and started to leave the room.

"Wait I don't understand what you're saying." Bernard looked the woman straight in the eye and said,

"Bill was no grass we killed him at his suggestion, we gave him a very quick death and it has left you money to survive with. The members of the Guild were very proud of what Bill did for us. Even though he was not a member, and to show their gratitude that packet on the table contains £40,000." with that Bernard walked out of the house down the street, turned a corner got into a car and was gone.

Chapter 38

THE GUILD NOW CONTROLLED over 90 per cent of the city; so far, they had left the drugs trade alone mainly for two reasons. The first being the fact that so much money was involved with drugs that the people running the various gangs that were dealing in it, were the hardest criminals that the City had to offer. The second reason was Max; Max really did not like the idea of connections with the drug trade. The Guild had many meetings about going into the drug trade and eventually Max had to let them have their way. That meant that the Guild would go into the drugs business. As normal, they had decided to go straight to the top, not for them starting at the bottom and gradually working their way to the top. The three Grandmasters had come to the decision that the only way to be in the drugs trade was to control it utterly.

The City appeared to be divided into bout six or seven patches, each one controlled by what was known as a drugs baron. The drugs business attracted a lot of publicity nearly every week the newspapers were running articles about one war or other involving disputes over gang ran territories. This meant that the police had to do something to show that they were earning their money. By abducting and question a few of the local pushers Max and his friends found that there was actually eight gangs, seven of which were the ones they kept making the papers and eighth one seemed to have a loose control over the others.

When the Guild acted, it was sudden without warning and the violence was terrific, all drug barons were hard violent men not averse to crippling or killing anybody that encroached on their territory. The chosen weapons of the Guild were the 9 mm Browning pistol and the 9 mm SMG that they had stolen from the army. Although the drug dealers were hard men, they had never had to contend with anybody with the sort of attitude that the Guild members had. This so-called Mr Big of the drugs trade was a dark skinned dark-haired black-eyed man called Angelo. Nobody knew him by any other name. Angelo was surrounded by mystery, it was rumoured that he was a member of a large Colombian family that was responsible for running drugs in every country in Europe. It was rumours like this that had kept him at the top of the pile; in fact it was rumours like this that he himself had spread throughout the underworld. The belief that he had connections, and the fact that he was a very violent temper man, all combined to make him the number one drugs Baron of the city. For years, the police had been trying to pin every drug crime that they could think of on this man, but so far, he had managed to weasel his way out of all them. Other drug barons did not know two things. First, he was no Colombian he was in fact a Jimmy Brown from the East end of London, his strange accent was all a sham. Secondly, the way he managed to weasel his way out of the police clutches was by informing on other gang members.

Angelo many years ago had bought an old farmhouse on the outskirts of the city, as he got more and more into drug dealing, so he had gradually turned the farmhouse into a strong house. In fact with an 8 ft wall surrounding the buildings and the small gatehouse at the entrance it was more like a fort. 24 hours a day seven days a week 52 weeks of the year two men sat at the Gate House making sure that only the right people got into the premises. With security, cameras mounted round the grounds Angelo considered that he was safe from all intrusions from outsiders. The only drugs that he allowed onto the premises were what people carried for their own personal use. He allowed none of staff to use drugs at all. If any of his staff needed disciplining or any of his own personal gang then it was always away from the buildings, after all he did not want any incriminating evidence where he was actually living. All the people that worked or lived within the perimeter walls were very heavily armed, and because of this, throughout the buildings Alberto had, had small secret hideaways made so that if the police raided his property by the time they had past the main gate everybody that was armed would have had time to lose their weapons. So far, Alberto's premises had been searched about six times and not once had any drugs or weapons been found by the police or their sniffer dogs.

Preparations for a large party that Angelo was throwing, for a few of the local high ranking police officers and local councillors, these were the ones that had already accepted his bribes but in his words "keep them sweet."

The two guards at the Gate House watched as the dark blue van approached down the driveway. They could see that two men sat in the front, one dressed in a white chef's jacket the other dressed as a waiter. As a van drew to a halt, one guard approached the driver's window, which the man in the white coat was winding-down. The other guard had started to open the gates. To the guards it was obvious that the van was something to do with the catering for the party. As the first guard came closer to the window, Max who was the driver said

"I've got something for you to taste if you want it?" The guard relaxed and smiled,

"That's fucking decent of you mate. They forget about us two out here." The second guard came round to the side of a van to see what was happening. Both men were now very relaxed, and they had both taken their hands from the pockets holding their pistols. They were now expecting something nice to eat. Max smiled and reached down to the side of his seat to fetch something. When his hand came up he was holding a 9 mm Browning pistol. The first Guards face registered shock and horror, he had time to see the knuckle on Max's index finger go white as a trigger was pulled, he almost saw the flame of the explosion as the bullet left the barrel. The bullet entered the guards face halfway up his nose and left the back of the guards head along with three quarters to the man's brain only to spread it over the front of the second guard. The gun fired a second time, and the other guard who had no time to react flew backwards when the bullet hit him in the sternum. Max jumped from the van and went to the second guard the man looked dead but to make sure Max put the muzzle of the gun between that man eyes and fired the third round. Max opened the side door of the van and two men jumped out, by time Max got back into the driver's seat of the van the two bodies had been dragged inside the gatehouse, and his two men were now in charge of the gate. The van drove carefully down the driveway round the front of the house and parked by the back door. The van doors were open and four men dressed as waiters stepped, out each one carrying a cardboard box. What couldn't be seen was the fact that not only were boxes empty but that the bottoms had been cut away and now each man with one hand at the boxes bottom the other one on top, the cardboard boxes concealed the sub-machineguns in each man's hand. Max opened the back door without knocking and announcing a loud voice.

"Hello Catering!" The four men in the kitchen were too busy with their game a cards so take much notice,

"Through that door, second right down the hall, first door on the left." One of the men said without even looking up. Max and the men with boxes did as told. This left Jake standing by the back door also holding a cardboard box, one of the card players looked up and said

"That for us, mate?"

"It sure is, I thought you deserve a treat." With that, Jake dropped the box and gently squeezed the trigger of his SMG. The hail of bullets took a four card players completely by surprise, blood and bone and tissue sprayed across the walls of the kitchen. Jake calmly turned and locked the kitchen door, as he started to walk through the house he could hear gunfire in other rooms as well as screams and pleading. As he went past the lounge, he could see two men and two women kneeling in front of the settee with one of the Guild members covering them with his SMG another stood in the doorway keeping guard.

In one of the bedrooms upstairs, Max found one naked man on a bed with two young women also naked, one ridding him and the other one sitting on his face. Both girls looked to be about fourteen years old, and both of them were out of their minds with drugs. A second man was filming them with a video camera Max shot the two women first, as they died both of their bowels relaxed, with a shout man underneath them came up splattering choking on a mouthful of one woman's shit. "Now you have got it right you fucking moron, eat shit before you die!" With that, Max put a bullet into the centre the man's stomach. Then he turned to the man using the camera,

"Keep the fucking camera on him; this is now going to be a snuff movie." The man nodded focusing the camera on the dying man on the bed.

"Zoom in for a close-up of his face, fill the screen." As the man nodded Max gun barked twice two small red holes appeared where dying man's pain filled eyes used to be. The back for a man's head exploded on to the pillow. The man with the camera suddenly felt a hot fluid running down his legs and he knew that he had pissed himself. He was staring straight into Max's eyes, as Max pointed the gun at him Max put a bullet into each of the man's knee caps, the man collapsed screaming on the floor pleading to be allowed to stay alive. Max lent over the man as he placed the muzzle of the SMG against the man's Adam's apple. Looking man straight in the eyes, he pressed the trigger twice. The two bullets shattered his spine just below the chin, almost parting his head from his body. In the lounge below this bedroom, the ceiling over Angelo's wife suddenly exploded through the plaster and the two now misshapen bullets ploughed into the top of Angelo wife's head which exploded like a ripe melon. The house was now in their control.

Chapter 39

THE TAKEOVER OF ANGELO'S business premises had gone smoothly and quietly. The mind of a truly violent man takes a lot of understanding. Max had planned a raid with the intention of killing everybody in the House. The death of Angelo's wife had been totally accidental, and although she was going to die anyway Max felt that he owed Angelo some sort of debt, so for the time being he let Angelo live. The Guild had piled the bodies into a small van, driven it down to the coast, and at low tide had been driven out as far as it could be driven, the contents covered in the oil and petrol and set alight. As this was a part of the coast that was seldom used by the public. The Guild hoped that the van and its contents would remain undiscovered for quite awhile.

Angelo gave up after a bit of persuasion the names of his contacts and suppliers; who when approached by the Guild were happy to work out a deal. The Guild now intended to takeover the rest of the drugs trade for the City. With their normal straight forward way of doing business, they decided that the only way was to takeover each gang all at the same time. The last thing they wanted was to have two or three gangs getting together and trying to fight back. So far they Guild taking over Angelo's premises had not been overly noticed by any of the public. The people that knew what has happened were part of the cities underworld and they had been shown enough and heard enough about the Guild to keep their mouths shut.

Each of the other seven gangs of drug dealers was cordially invited to attend a meeting. The invitation actually went some thing like,

"The two top people of the gang will be in the Blue Feather at 8:30 pm on this coming Monday. Each person than attends will have with them £5,000 in used notes. We the Guild are asking you very nicely to be there." Not one gang leader or his number two even for one second considered not going. This was the power and the fear that the local criminals now had of the Guild.

8:30 pm on the Monday evening, 14 very hard tough-looking men sat in the saloon bar of the Blue Feathers. These people did not mix as a social crowd; many of them had fought over parts of the town considered their patch. Each man had £5,000 in used notes on his person and each man was carrying some sort of firearm. 25 minutes to nine the door to the saloon bar opened and a young pleasant faced man entered. Appearances can be very deceptive, Tandy walked through the crowded room until he stood with his back against the bar. In a nice pleasant voice he said

"Good evening gentleman I have come to escort you to a party, please follow me." With that, he walked back out of the room and waited on the pavement beside the open doors of a coach, as the men came out he directed them to get into the coach and to remain quiet. When the men were all on the coach, the doors shut the coach pulled away. They did not stop until they reached a farmhouse on the outskirts of the city. The farm belonged to one of the members of the Guild. As they got off the coach they was ushered into a small barn, here they were all handed a drink as they entered. The barn was clean and tidy and there were 14 chairs laid out in a semi-circle they was laid out in such a way only two chairs were together in any one place. That way each gang leader and his number two sat together; with out having to be too close to any of the other gang leaders. Max Jake and Rab walked into the barn and stood in front of the 14 men. Max opened the meeting by thanking each of them by name for attending. He then said.

"Gentlemen in a few moments we will be going into the house, and understanding your business and the rivalry between each group of you I would like you to pay me and my comrades a courtesy. I would like you to all stand and remove all your weapons, by weapons I do mean fire arms, knives, knuckle-dusters and even packets of rolled-up coins, I would like you to put these weapons on the chairs. They naturally will be returned to you when you leave." The men hesitated, after all nobody wanted to be without protection, yet on the other hand, none of them wished to argue with the Guild. The men put their weapons on their chairs. Then they were led out of the barn towards the farmhouse. At the door Rab stood with a metal detector as each man entered the house Rab quickly run the machine over them, and it shows the men's fear of the Guild that not one of them had tried to conceal a weapon. Inside the main room of the House, a large table had been laid out and the men were seated, more drinks were passed round and the men started to relax a little.

Max Jake and Rab joined the men at the table, again Max opened the conversation by saying,

"Gentlemen I will not waste your valuable time as I know you will not waste mine. You may or may not know that the Guild has taken over Angelo's, shall we say, contacts we are now going to be your sole suppliers. This is not going to be an if or but. It is a fact." As he said this, the door opened and Tandy walked into the room.

"This gentleman is Tandy; you have already met him once tonight. As from today he is your boss, you will answer directly to him. Now I know this has come as a bit of an unpleasant surprise to you, so I have a proposition for you. Each of you has about your person £5,000, that as it happens is the entrance fee to join the Guild. What I am offering now is a chance to join the Guild." The 14 men that sat round the table were absolutely stunned, first they had had a very profitable business snatched away from under their noses and in the next moment, they were offered a chance to pay a lot of money and join the very firm that was taking their business away from them. The fear of the Guild was of such magnitude that the 14 men sat round the table, all of them were considered hard, most of them had been responsible for either maiming or killing rivals and people that upset them. Some of them had damaged people just for the fun of it, but not one man dared stand-up or start to shout or even complain. One of the bosses sat back and half raised his hand like a schoolchild.

"£5,000 to join your Guild from what I've heard that is not all, that needs doing is it?" Tandy looked the man up and down,

"You obviously know what the rules are along with the money you will have to be videoed killing somebody, that is why nobody grasses on the Guild." He then looked round the room his eyes come to rest on each man.

"We don't have all day as you gentlemen know time is money, those of you that want to join stand-up now." Out of the 14 men, three bosses and four second-in-commands stood up. Max nodded to Tandy then he looked at the standing men and told them to go out the door. The men went out, they were led to another room where three bottles of whisky sat on the table: with 14 glasses. The men were told to sit down and relax for a while and it was suggested that as they were joining the Guild all old quarrels between them should be forgotten.

In the other room the whisky bottle was passed round and the other seven men were given a large drink. Max sat at the head off the table looking at the remaining men.

"Gentlemen I am looking at my watch, I will wait five minutes in that time I would like you to consider changing your minds. I will not force any man or woman into joining the Guild it has to be voluntary."

At the end of five minutes, one second-in-command stood up and said.

"I think I'll join." When the door opened, again five armed men stepped into the room, the remaining men were told to stand and their thumbs were joined with cable ties behind their backs each one of them was then blindfold and gagged. They were led out and pushed into the back of a large van. The van drove off as the new recruits were led out of the farmhouse and were told to board the coach again. The van and coach drove steadily along the side roads for the next three hours until they came to a large field with a small bunch of trees in the middle, here the coach stopped. 20 minutes later the van drove up and seven men removed from the back of it. One of the men was a bit unlucky he had just come out of a pub, was blind drunk when a van stopped next to him and the driver said.

"Would you like a lift mate?" The man was bundled in the back to the van, tied up blindfold and gagged like the rest of them. The Guild needed seven men in that van. The men from the van were led across a field to the small bunch of trees, under the eyes of the Guild members that accompanied them they were stripped and tied with their backs to separate trees. They were still blindfold and gagged.

One by one, the new would be members were taken from the coach walked across to the trees where they found a very bright light set up above a video camera and a man tied to a tree. When the man's blindfold and gag were removed, the new recruit was handed a Browning 9 mm pistol containing one round he was then placed in front of the bound man, his arm was lifted until he held the pistol barrel between the man's eyes, he was then told to press the trigger. That night the Guild acquired eight new members.

Chapter 40

THE GUILD NOW HAD the City totally stitched up. There was no crime that in one way or the other did not involve the Guild, every crime that was committed put money into the Guilds coffers. Any crime that did happen without the Guilds say-so was punishable by death.

The crime figures for the City actually went down mostly because petty crime became nearly outdated.

The drugs trade brought so much money into the Guild that money became nothing special, but with the Guild taking over the drugs trade the drugs cut all to the same standard, the amount of deaths by druggies taking badly cut and mixed drugs was right down. With the Guild controlling the clubs and pubs massage parlours brothels and all the other dens of iniquity, fights became less frequent, the red light area didn't hit the headlines in the papers quite so often and everything seemed to be going nicely. The police feared the Guild as much as the criminals did but because the crime figures were down they just let the Guild get on with it. After all, as far as local criminals were concerned the Guild was doing a better job of keeping them in line than the police had done, and the police could grab all the credit for it.

A couple of years after the complete takeover of the city the three Grandmasters sat in a very smart hotel having a drink and a dinner. Jake had been fiddling about all evening, and eventually Rab looked at him and snapped

"Jake, what the fucking hell is the matter with you?" Jake looked rather sheepish,

"Before I met Max I had nothing, you and Max have turned my whole life around. The trouble is for the last two years all we have done is sit back, take money and naturally spend it. I miss the excitement, we three sat down and decided to take over a whole city and we did it. Now we've got nothing left to get excited over."

Max looked at the other two

"I understand what Jake is talking about. I have just had an idea."

"Let's take on another city."

The three men looked at each other raised their glasses and grinned.

The end

Printed in the United Kingdom by
Lightning Source UK Ltd., Milton Keynes
139206UK00001B/48/P